CLAIMED BY THE ALIEN WARRIOR

HOPE HART

CHAPTER ONE

N*evada*

"Move that back leg."

I adjust, nodding as I switch to a slightly more comfort-able fighting stance.

The only difference between fighting on Agron and fighting on Earth?

The sword in my hand.

That hand trembles, and I scowl. Turns out my wrists are nowhere near as strong as they should be if I'm planning to wield a sword on this planet.

The Braxians are bigger than me, stronger than me, tougher than me, and usually faster than me.

The good news? I'm not planning to fight Braxians.

I'm going after the Voildi. They're still bigger than us humans, but if I'm smart, I might at least have a chance.

"Okay," Asroz says. "What are your three rules?"

"Strike first, think smart, and fight dirty."

He nods. For whatever reason, Asroz has decided to train me. Most of the warriors here were amused and then appalled when I started learning how to fight with a sword. I think Asroz is also amused, but in his words, if I'm determined to learn, he may as well prevent me from waving my sword around like an asshole.

Okay, those weren't his exact words.

I can barely lift the giant swords that these warriors carry. So Asroz kindly gave me a training sword. Yesterday, he finally sharpened it, and in theory, I should be ready to go.

Yeah, right.

We're practicing with wooden swords for now, which is good 'cause otherwise I'd probably have lost more than one limb already.

"Why will you strike first?" Asroz asks.

"Because I need the element of surprise. No one will expect a woman to be any good with a sword. And once they decide to cut me down, I don't have the muscle strength to absorb the force of an overhead blow."

"Think smart?"

"Only attack if necessary. Plan, lay traps, and use my surroundings."

"Good. And why will you fight dirty?"

I grin. Truthfully, I don't know how to fight any other way.

"I've got hand-to-hand combat experience—something many creatures here don't have. They're used to relying on their swords. A hit to the nuts hurts the same whether you're human or Voildi."

"Good."

I've been surprised by how seriously Asroz is taking this training. Most people assume he's just indulging me, but he's not an idiot. He knows I'm planning to go after our friends. And he's hoping to give me the best possible chance of coming out alive.

"Time for your drills."

I nod, ready. Unlike one would probably expect, most of my drills don't involve using my sword at all. Instead, they're all about speed. On this planet, the fact that I'm light on my feet is about all I've got going for me.

Unlike what I expected after a lifetime of watching Hollywood movies, blocking a sword is my last line of defense. Asroz has taught me some fancy footwork, and the goal is that I simply won't be there when a sword is aimed at my head.

I raise my sword, and Asroz attacks. I've got a feeling he's still nowhere near to using his full speed, but I'm definitely getting faster.

His strikes come one after the other, and I dodge, weave, and pivot, gradually moving backward until I can duck under his arm.

My sword comes up, and I slide it along his ribs. He stops and grins at me, pleased.

"Point," he says. "But that should have been a thrust. I was off-balance, and my heart was right there."

I blow out a breath. I'm a marine. I've seen combat. I've killed before. But the idea of sliding a sword into someone's heart doesn't come naturally.

"This needs to be instinct," Asroz says, and I nod. Just like when fighting a guy who outweighs me on Earth, I have to be brutal. Flesh wounds are just going to annoy anyone who's attacking me.

And since the Voildi are usually in packs, I don't have time to fuck around.

Sweat is dripping in my eyes by the time we're finished,

and I turn, not at all surprised to find an audience. Men outnumber women on this planet by ten to one, and the women? They wear dresses.

If I were running in a floor-length dress, I'd be guaranteed to faceplant.

The people here aren't shy about staring, and while I used to make a point of meeting each of their gazes, now I just tend to ignore them.

The reason for the scandalized looks currently coming my way? The leather pants I'm wearing. Honestly, I'm not sure what offends the locals more—the sword in my hand, my filthy mouth, or the pair of Braxian pants I stole. Luckily, the seamstress seemed to find my request hilarious, and she's currently working on another pair for me, along with some shirts.

I'd kill for a bath right about now. Sure, I'd rather shower, but you take what you can get in this place. I wipe sweat off my forehead with the back of my hand, once again ignoring the eyes on me as I make my way to the mishua pen.

No point getting clean when I'm about to be working with the mishua.

This is my "punishment."

A few days ago, I had a minor freak-out. I decided I couldn't take the waiting around anymore and attempted to sneak out of the camp.

Truthfully, I'm glad I was caught. No, I didn't enjoy the chewing out I was given by Rakiz, the tribe king, but leaving unprepared is a bad idea. I was planning to go on foot but quickly realized my mistake: I need to move faster.

I eye the mishua as I get closer. They're not the most attractive beasts, but they can cover more ground in a few hours than I can in an entire day of walking. They're intelligent, dangerous, and moody as fuck.

But you know what? So am I.

Mishua don't tolerate females riding them. Personally, I wonder if it's a chicken-and-egg situation. Maybe they're just not used to females, since the women around here wouldn't dream of riding alone.

Rakiz's voice runs through my head as I open the pen and stride inside.

"You want to dress like a male and fight like a male? Fine. You can also work like a male. You will work with the mishua until I believe you have learned your lesson."

I promised him he'd regret that decision. And it turns out that working with the mishua is good for me in two ways. First, it's helping to strengthen my forearms and wrists, which is exactly what I need to wield a sword. But more importantly, I have the perfect opportunity to convince a mishua to let me sit on its back.

"Hi, girls," I say as I stride through the pen. The mishua have gotten used to me already and pay me little attention, although a few of them snort at me as I get close.

When the Braxians saved us from the Voildi, I took one look at their mishua and dubbed them *dino-horses.* They're lizard-looking dark-green creatures with mouthfuls of sharp fangs, horns covering their snouts, and huge heads. Oh, and weirdly, the bottoms of their legs are covered in thick fur.

The mishua have intimidating red eyes and bad attitudes. They're fierce in battle and can travel long distances without needing a break.

I'm pretty sure they can't understand English, but I've been talking to them anyway, hoping they'll get used to the sound of my voice.

"I'm getting better with the sword," I tell one of them,

and she stares at me for a moment, red eyes glinting, before she turns, giving me an up close look at leather, green mishua-ass.

Yeah, it's tough going. But no worse than the popular girls in high school.

Weirdly, the mishua that pays me the most attention happens to be Rakiz's preferred mount. She's bigger than the rest, and her eyes hold an intelligence that's more than a little disconcerting.

"Hey, Racia. Wow, bet you're bored in here, huh?"

She stares at me as I get closer, snorting at me in warning, and I stop in my tracks.

"Wow, someone's pissy today. Probably cause you haven't been out for a while. When *was* the last time you went out anyway?" I tut, shaking my head as if saddened. "It's such a shame the king is always hanging around at camp. You must get so bored."

On the off chance that the mishua can understand me, I want to sow the seeds that will one day make her tolerate me on her back.

I turn and mosey on over to the sleeping area, where I've stowed the huge shovel I was given. My task? Mucking out the mishua pen.

The tribe was astounded to hear about my punishment, and I've even caught regret in Rakiz's eyes once or twice. But he'll never go back on his word, and he may think this is the worst task I've ever done, but it's not even close.

My uncle had horses when I was a kid, and he always made me muck out the stables in exchange for a ride. Poop doesn't bother me. Although, these huge creatures produce more of it than any animal I've ever seen.

I lean over, ignoring the eyes on me as I get to work. The

people here like to stare. I get it—I'm different. But it's hard to plan my escape when I'm being watched like a hawk.

The good news? There are fewer people leaning against the fence than there were yesterday. Hopefully these people will get bored soon as well.

While I can block out most of the attention, one hard gaze is more difficult to ignore. I look up as Rakiz walks past, his council trailing in his steps, and I sneer at him as he nods at me.

Rakiz may be the tribe king, but as I've told him before, that doesn't mean he's *my* king.

His eyes lighten with amusement, and I turn away. For whatever reason, out of all the huge warriors here, Rakiz is the one that makes my thighs clench.

I just don't get it.

He's bossy and overbearing and refuses to take me seriously. Due to the shortage of females on this planet, the males here seem to think that females should be coddled and protected.

When I tried to explain that I was more than capable of helping to look for our friends, Rakiz did everything but pat me on the head.

And then he had the gall to be furious when I decided to go on my own.

Shoveling shit gives me a lot of time to myself. Unfortunately, that means I have a lot of hours to think about my life on Earth.

I can't stand the idea that everyone will think I went AWOL. I was on leave, visiting my friend Kat, when I went for a walk to get some air.

That's the last thing I remember.

It was late at night, and I was wearing shorts and a tank top—more than most of the other women, the majority of whom were taken from their beds. I had my car keys and phone, and I hope to God someone found them deserted somewhere and everyone knows I was taken and that I didn't just leave.

I'd never go AWOL on purpose.

I can't think about that now. My focus has to be on finding the other women so we can get the hell off this planet.

***

Rakiz

I almost laugh as Nevada glowers at me. The human female is currently cleaning out the mishua pen, yet she still looks as arrogant as ever.

Something about this female calls to me—even though every time I spend more than a few moments in her presence, I feel the urge to shake some sense into her.

The punishment I gave her has not been well received by my tribe. Surprisingly, it is the females who have supported it the most. My warriors, however, are mostly shocked that I would give a female such physical work.

My reasoning was that Nevada would be so tired at the end of each day that she would no longer have the energy to make the kinds of plans that will get her killed.

Unfortunately, the hellion simply began training earlier with Asroz, and I strongly suspect she considers her work in the mishua pen to be an extension of her workout.

I almost groan as Nevada bends over, her well-toned ass flexing in her pants. Numerous females have demanded that I take those pants away, but watching Nevada stalk through the camp with leather hugging her long legs is one of the few pleasures I have. I'd be an idiot to take them from her.

Plus, she would likely attempt to castrate me.

I sigh as my councilors start again.

"Really, your majesty, I just think—"

"Enough." I hold up a hand, wishing for nothing more than some peace and quiet. Truthfully, I'd rather be working in the mishua pen with Nevada than listening to the councilors' complaints.

"You have more than enough time to bring these concerns to me during our meetings. Why must you follow me around camp each day like children following their mother?"

Silence surrounds me, and I sigh. I am growing short-tempered. The fact that a single female is responsible for my bad mood is not lost on me.

After her escape attempt, I ordered Nevada to sleep in my tashiv, which is the most guarded place in the camp. She refused until I threatened to tie her to me while I slept. Now, she creeps into her furs on the other side of the room each night once she believes I am already asleep. Then she creeps back out before the sun rises each morning.

This morning, I didn't even wake when she left.

My guards have been ordered to stop her if she attempts to leave again at night. Unfortunately, I don't trust the hellion's current good behavior at all.

I scowl as the councilor starts up again and move back toward my tashiv. I tune him out as I walk, nodding to my warriors as they head toward the training arena.

How can I convince the stubborn female that to leave this camp would be suicide? She believes that I'm not working to find her friends when my every decision is based on freeing up more of my warriors to hunt for the other females.

It still stuns me that such small females are here on our planet. If my men hadn't seen their spaceship with their own eyes, I would struggle to believe that it exists. Unfortunately, as soon as the females landed, a pack of Voildi discovered the ship and convinced the females that they were saving them. The Voildi were leading them to certain death when Terex—the leader of my warriors—located them.

Now, four of the females are still missing—three of them likely still in the hands of the Voildi and one taken by Dragix, our great ancestor.

Our tribe is down to three human females, with the one known as Alexis choosing to exchange her freedom for information about the lost female. She has chosen to stay with Dexar, a warrior who can only sometimes be trusted.

My body tenses at the thought. When Asroz told me that one of the females had stayed...

I marched to my mishua, ready to drag Nevada back by her hair if I had to. It was a possessive, irrational reaction, and I still don't understand it.

Neither do I understand the way I buried my hand in the stubborn female's lush hair and took her mouth when I realized she had returned.

To me.

CHAPTER TWO

N *evada*

You know what's good about being smaller than most people here?

It's easier to sneak around.

On Earth, I'm on the tall side for a woman, coming in at five feet nine. Here? Everyone towers over me. The women have a foot on me, and the men? Even more. It's like I woke up in a land of giants.

Usually this doesn't please me. But today, the fact that I only come up to most warriors' chests makes it easier for me to blend in.

"I heard they were taken to Nexia to be sold," a warrior says, pouring another drink.

My chest clenches at the thought. We were already sold once—to horned purple aliens who crashed their ship, leaving us stranded here. Truthfully, that crash was probably better than whatever those assholes had lined up for us.

"Rakiz has already sent Tagiz and Hewex to make sure the slave market is still dismantled," the warrior continues.

I've heard about the slave market. With females being so rare on this planet, we're targeted by almost everyone. Leaving this camp is a risk, but it's a risk I have to take.

Apparently it was Dexar who dismantled the slave market. He's the one who held onto the information we needed until Alexis agreed to stay with him.

I barely hold back a snort, not wanting to reveal my eavesdropping. Alexis knows we're coming back for her. Not only would I never leave without every woman who landed here, but as a mechanical engineer, she's our best hope of fixing the ship we arrived in.

But where's Nexia?

I have a map I've been working on using ceptri, which is similar to charcoal, and a piece of material. Each time I hear something I can use, I sneak back to the kradi I shared with Vivian and Alexis and add it to my map.

The other warrior snorts. "It may have been dismantled, but why would they be traveling through the Seinex Forest if they didn't have to?"

The Seinex Forest? Where have I heard that before?

Shit, I can't remember.

I mentally add it to my list and vow to ask someone about it later. Most of the warriors know exactly what I'm up to and won't answer my questions—even Asroz. Oh, he knows what I'm planning, and I think the only reason he teaches me how to use a sword is so he'll feel a little less guilt if I'm killed.

I look up at the sky and scowl. Rakiz has declared that I have to be back in his stupid hut by sundown. Having a curfew really grinds my gears, but I'm playing nice. For now.

Thankfully, the days are long here right now, but the curfew still cuts down on the amount of time I have to eavesdrop on Rakiz's warriors when they're relaxing after a long day. Their tongues are looser later on in the night when they've had more noptri—a drink similar to alcohol.

While it's a shame I can't hang around, at least I have my secret weapon to help.

I duck into Vivian's kradi on my way back to Rakiz's hut. She's picking at her nails and smiles as she looks up.

Vivian's beautiful, and she knows it. Unfortunately, she's also someone who tends to lash out at those she considers weaker than herself.

I'm not one of those people, but our friend Ellie is. Regret occasionally crosses Vivian's face when I mention Ellie's name, and I'm pretty sure she feels bad for the way she acted when we first arrived.

As she should.

"Hey, Nevada, what's up?"

"Not much. Hey, listen, what have you heard about the Seinex Forest?"

She frowns while I move to my hiding place and unearth my map.

"Isn't that the place the dragon was last seen?"

Triumph hits me. "That's it. I knew I'd heard it before. Dexar mentioned it when we went to ask him for information." I stare at my map. "Do me a favor. Find out everything you can about Nexia."

Vivian nods, looking curiously at my map. "Anything else?"

"The usual. Find out where most of Rakiz's warriors are located and which areas they're searching."

She grins. "More flirting with the giant warriors? Sure."

I smirk. Most people assume Vivian is exactly as she appears. If they paid attention, though, they'd realize that all that flirting and gossiping is for one reason and one reason only.

To find our friends.

For all her bitchiness, Vivian wants to find the other women as much as I do. And she sure as hell wants to get back to Earth. It almost killed her to stay behind when we went looking for news of Charlie and the other women, but while we were gone, she collected most of the information I'm using for my map.

"Thanks, Viv."

"No problem. I wish I could go with you."

"Same. But it's better for me to go alone. I need you to keep gathering information in case I'm caught."

She nods, but her gaze moves away.

"I know you'd rather come," I say. "But these guys trust you."

Her mouth twists. "Because they assume I'm an idiot who is only interested in what my dress looks like."

"Yeah," I say honestly. "Because you were smart enough to act that way so I could figure out where the hell we are. Teamwork makes the dream work."

She smiles again, and this time it reaches her eyes. Then she leans forward and pokes her head out of the kradi.

"It's getting dark," she warns me, laughing at my scowl. "You still haven't climbed on that warrior?"

I shake my head. "Nope." I pop the *p*, and Vivian raises her brow.

"Even after that kiss?"

That kiss.

The one that Rakiz laid on me the moment I got back

from Dexar's territory. Later, I learned that he thought that I was the one who stayed behind. And he was ready to go after me himself—sending shock waves through the entire tribe.

Apparently the king leaving camp alone simply isn't done. If he gets killed, Terex is next in line, and while he's popular and well liked, everyone knows he doesn't want to rule. That means that there would be a power vacuum, infighting, and at the very least, an outcry that the king could possibly leave his people to fend for themselves.

I roll my eyes at the thought even as a warm feeling rises in my chest. He was going to risk that for me.

"That kiss was his way of punishing me for going. He knew I'd hate the attention."

Vivian tilts her head. "I don't think so. But go on and bury your head in the sand if you have to."

"I do."

I glance toward the sky and sigh, muttering my goodbye as I leave the kradi.

Unfortunately, Rakiz is still up when I arrive. I prefer to crawl into my bed when he's fast asleep on the other side of the room.

He looks up from sharpening his sword, his chest bare and those incredible scales catching the light.

When I study the way those muscles move, it's easy to see how these people could be descended from dragons.

"You're late," he says, and I wrinkle my nose at him.

"I need a bath."

He flashes his teeth at me. "You do indeed."

Arana walks in, her eyes crinkling at the corners when she looks at me.

"Oh dear," she says. "I'll fill the bath."

I hate the idea of other people serving me.

"I can do it," I offer, and she glances at Rakiz, who shakes his head.

"You know the rules."

I narrow my eyes at him. "When are you going to let me go back to my kradi?"

He stretches, and it takes all my willpower to keep my eyes on his face.

"When I feel you are smart enough to understand why you can't leave this camp by yourself."

Arana smiles at me. "I've left your evening food by the fire." She nods toward it. "Why don't you eat? Your bath will be ready when you're done."

I open my mouth to protest, but when Rakiz flicks his eyes to me, I sigh and simply nod.

Truthfully, I'm exhausted. After a long day of training and then mucking out the mishua pen, I want nothing more than to fill my belly and then slide into some warm water.

I sit across from Rakiz and take my plate. I've always had a healthy appetite, and the food here is better than one would think. Arana is an excellent cook, and she's always slipping me a piece of fruit or a sweet cake between meals.

Rakiz makes me uncomfortable in a way that few men make me uncomfortable. Half the time, I want to kill him. But the other half...I can barely resist the urge to jump his bones. He's huge, but he moves like the perfect predator. A few days ago, I watched him training, and to my complete mortification, the sight of him in his element, a savage grin on his face, a sword in his hand...

I instantly dampened.

The first thing I'm doing when I get back to Earth? Getting laid.

I must be desperate if I'm eyeing up the same man who treats me like a child, coddles me, and gives me stupid rules.

He seems to think that simply being born with a dick means that he can tell me what to do.

"How was your work today?"

I almost ignore him, but there's no one else to talk to. Let him think he has me where he wants me.

"Fine."

He stretches, and I move my gaze back to the fire. Soon we won't need to light one anymore, and the entire camp will move to a new location. I'm planning to be on my way back to Earth before that happens.

"The moment you apologize and swear on your honor that you won't leave this camp, you can stop working with the mishua."

I know this. Unfortunately, I'll eat dirt before I apologize, and I've made my feelings about staying here clear.

"I don't understand why you won't just let me go. Send me with the next group of warriors who take up the search."

"It's not happening."

"News flash, buddy, you're not in charge of me."

"In this tribe, I'm in charge of everyone."

Sometimes I see hints of humor in his eyes as if he's almost laughing at himself. That doesn't stop me from grinding my teeth at his high-handedness though.

Arana reappears. "Oh, you're finished. Good. Your bath is ready, Nevada."

"Thank you," I say, getting to my feet. I ignore the heated look in Rakiz's eyes and move into the bathing room.

CHAPTER THREE

R *akiz*

I ALMOST GROAN AS THE HELLION GETS TO HER FEET, THOSE long legs striding into my bathing room, where she'll take off her clothes and splash in the water until I'm almost out of my mind with need.

Listening to Nevada take her bath is my favorite part of the day.

Her sighs and groans as she slides into the water?

Bliss.

I can barely resist the urge to stalk into the bathing room and climb into the bath with her.

I feel my lips curl at the thought. She would likely gut me if I tried.

Sometimes she mutters to herself while bathing. I've heard the words "arrogant fucking asshole" on more than one occasion.

She is the most frustrating, infuriating, stubborn female I have ever met. But when she is close...I am never bored.

My father raised me to be thankful for my crown. To appreciate the trust my people have in me and recognize the importance of putting the tribe's needs before my own. Before he died, I was a true warrior, known for my fearlessness in battle. I was most content when riding far from the camp, hunting Voildi and keeping our people safe from threats.

The moment he died, that life ended.

In some ways, I understand Nevada's need to be free. I have the same need.

But we don't always get what we need.

I barely hold back a growl as I hear Nevada's clothes drop to the floor. She says something to Arana, who laughs, likely promising to clean her pants.

Those pants...

I listen intently, cock hardening as Nevada slides into the water, a tiny moan leaving her lips. She gasps as she dunks her head, and then I'm treated to the sound of splashing as she washes her body and hair.

She's efficient, rarely spending longer than a few minutes in the water. If she were my female, I would teach her to relax, basking with her in the water while I massaged that gloriously toned body.

I shake my head at the thought, getting to my feet and striding to the door. I open it, letting in some fresh air while I look out at my people.

Eventually I will have to take a mate. To rule by my side, she will need to be pleasant and agreeable, popular and kind. My councilors remind me daily that if I were to fall, I would have no heir to take my place.

I grind my teeth. I have known all the females in this

tribe since before I could hold a sword. It's not uncommon for rulers on this planet to arrange to swap unmated females between tribes. Truthfully, I know one or two females who would be willing to travel to Dexar's tribe with the hope of finding a mate there. Dexar would then return the favor.

One day, such a thing will happen. As my father taught me, I must always think of the good of the tribe.

I close the door and move into my sleeping room while I attempt to ignore the sound of Nevada getting out of her bath. Water will be running down her body even as she pats the drops from her skin, then she'll change into her sleep clothes—a shirt she lifted from my closet.

If the sight of her dressed in my shirt fills me with savage pleasure, I don't let her see it.

I slide off my pants and climb between my furs, pulling them over me as Nevada walks in, ignoring my presence.

She climbs into her own furs, and a tiny groan leaves her throat. I bet she is sore after such a long day of physical activity, and I take a moment to imagine the moans that would leave her lips as I kneaded the knots out of her tense muscles.

I sigh and roll onto my back, staring at the ceiling as I prepare for another sleepless night.

***

Nevada

I add another shovel of poop to my mountain. I'd never let Rakiz know, but I'm enjoying the physical activity.

Better than sitting around in a dress anyway.

When the Arcav invaded Earth, I prepared to go to war. But I could never have imagined the firepower and technology the alien race had. Within two months, all of us had implants in our ears so we could understand other alien races, and women were giving blood samples to determine if they could be mates to the Arcav.

If I weren't a marine, I would have gone into hiding.

Thankfully I wasn't genetically compatible as a mate.

"You know, I feel sorry for you," I murmur to Racia as I shovel. The mishua looks on, standing closer than the other mishua, who prefer to pretend I don't exist most of the time.

Racia lifts her head, eyeing me. Is that eye narrowed slightly in offense?

"It's just that...all the other mishua get to go have adventures. What do you get? The occasional ride for exercise. That's it. All I'm saying is that must really suck. I'd understand if you thought about leaving sometimes. I think about it too."

Racia stares at me for a long moment and then goes back to eating the grains and meat the mishua prefer.

I hold back a laugh. I've been working on her every day. No one would ever accuse me of being subtle.

When the Braxians first found us, they put me on a mishua named Leai, making sure to tie her to the mishua that Asroz was riding. She tolerated me on her back only because I wasn't actually steering her anywhere.

Since I've been here, I've tried to make friends with her, figuring that since I've already ridden her once, she'd be the most likely to let me ride her again.

I couldn't be more wrong. The mishua loathes me. While most of them ignore me, Leai actively hates me, attempting to bite and gore me whenever I step into the pen. A few days ago, it finally got to the stage where the warriors had to separate her from the pack whenever I was working in the pen.

Now all my eggs are in Racia's basket. At the very least, the mishua occasionally appears to find me interesting.

"Wow, it stinks."

I turn as Ellie arrives, gagging. Her face pales as she opens her mouth, turning her head to suck in some fresh air.

"Yeah, no shit." I smirk, and she grins back while we examine the huge mountain of poop I've created.

"How are you?" she asks.

"Better than you'd think." I wipe the back of my hand across my forehead, and from the look on Ellie's face, that hand wasn't as clean as I thought it was.

She wrinkles her nose in horror, and we both crack up.

"God, who would've thought that this would be how I'd end up on an alien planet?" I say, reaching up to wipe at my eyes.

"Ew. No. Let me."

Ellie steps forward, using her sleeve and preventing me from smearing who knows what on my face.

"How was the mating ceremony?" I ask. We were all invited, but I preferred to work on my technique with my sword. These people have been gracious hosts since we arrived, but the last thing I need is to start forming relationships here. I need to keep my eye on the prize.

"It was good. I wish you had come."

I shrug. "I had things to do."

"What kind of things?"

I send her a look. I don't think Ellie will approve of my plans.

"I'm going after Beth, Ivy, and Zoey. I've been eavesdropping and collecting information, and after our visit to the Krazion tribe, I've got a pretty good idea of where they would've been taken."

Ellie bites her lower lip, something she only does when she's anxious or nervous. "It's so dangerous, Nevada."

I nod. "I know. I'm not an idiot, Ellie. I know it's not the best idea I've ever had. But here's the thing. I've got food, clean water, clothes, and somewhere to sleep. No one's planning to eat me or sell me or anything else. We can't say the same for the other women. I can't just sit around here and do nothing."

Her brow creases. "I'll come with you."

I don't think so. "You've done enough. It's because of you that we have the information we do. And no offense, Ellie, but you're useless in a fight."

She sighs. "What if I convinced Terex to help? We could all go."

"Don't say a word to him," I say, narrowing my eyes. "He'll tell Rakiz, and then I won't be going anywhere. You know that asshole is making me sleep in his hut? He decided he wants to keep an eye on me." I scowl, annoyed all over again, and lean against my shovel. "I'm still deciding whether to take a bath after I'm finished here. As much as I'm dreaming of clean water, I'd love to stink up his place."

"You're both as bad as each other." A smirk dances around her mouth, and I laugh. She's not wrong.

"Look, Ellie, I'm experienced in the outdoors. Okay, this planet's different, but the basic rules apply." I sigh, checking to make sure there aren't any curious ears listening in. "Right before the Arcav invaded, I was a prisoner of war in Baghdad. The only thing that got me through was knowing that someone would be coming for me. They weren't going to leave me behind."

I glance away. Even the thought of that time in my life makes me tense, and I push down the memories that tend to climb on top of each other. I've been so exhausted since I got here that I've barely dreamed, but the occasional flashback still hits when I least expect it.

Ellie scowls, drawing me from my thoughts. "Are you seriously going to leave me with Vivian?"

I laugh. "She's not that bad. Honestly, I feel sorry for her."

"Yeah, her life must be so hard." Ellie's voice is dripping with sarcasm, and I eye her.

"Vivian has obviously been taught that her only worth is connected to how she looks. You and I know better. And on this planet, her looks will only get her so far. We're all aliens here." I grin at the thought. "Now are you with me?"

"Fine," she says with a sigh. "How can I help?"

CHAPTER FOUR

N*evada*

I'VE FALLEN INTO SOMEWHAT OF A TRUCE WITH THE TRIBE king. Rakiz is the only one around to talk to after a long day, and these days, he stays up waiting for me, asking me questions about my life on Earth while I eat my evening meal.

I think he's lonely.

I get it. During the day, everyone wants a piece of him. They're knocking on his door first thing in the morning, and they don't stop until Arana shoos them away when the sun goes down. Someone always wants something—whether it's permission to hunt, a blessing for their mating, a resolution between feuding families...the tribe king never gets a moment of peace.

He seems to be closest to Terex, but even Terex leaves occasionally, and he's pretty much shacked up with Ellie now. Terex is also in charge of the warriors, overseeing training, and delegating men and weapons.

A few days ago, in a moment of weakness, I even found myself defending the guy. As if the tribe king needs my help.

I was getting a late start on the day, since Asroz couldn't train me that morning. A knock on the door sounded while I was pulling on my boots, and I rolled my eyes when Arana opened the door, revealing two young warriors who were petitioning Rakiz to be able to begin training with the adults.

"Maybe you would have a better chance if you waited until the king has finished eating his breakfast, hmm?" I asked, and Arana's mouth fell open while the boys spluttered, reddening as they backed out the door.

Rakiz grinned. "Fierce female," he murmured, his eyes heating.

I stalked straight out the door, unsure why I'd felt the need to step in.

Now it's time to leave this camp behind. And I'm shaking as I think about what's going to happen next.

I'm lying awake, staring at the ceiling. In a few minutes, I'll need to get up and get ready as if it's a normal day.

The good thing about being hated by most of the women here? They're willing to help me leave if it'll mean that I'm no longer sleeping in the king's tashiv.

Two days ago, I stopped in at the seamstress's kradi. Eres is a hardworking woman with a daughter my age. A daughter who I'm pretty sure Eres would like to be queen. The seamstress handed me a pile of clothes, including a pair of her mate's old leather pants, which she'd adjusted for me. Now I have a full wardrobe with enough changes of clothes to get me through weeks of travel.

"Here you go," she said, handing me the clothes. "Be careful."

"I don't know what you're talking about," I said, and she

gave me a rare smile before adding an incredibly soft blanket to the pile.

I get up, making sure my clothes are ready to grab later. Rakiz's eyes meet mine, and I almost blush as his gaze scans my form.

So what if I'm wearing his shirt? It's not like there are any pajamas around here.

Rakiz's dark gaze tells me he likes what he sees, and I turn away as he stretches, leaning down to grab his pants. I'm well aware that the guy sleeps naked, and I have to keep my eyes from wandering over in his direction whenever his furs slip low, revealing the tantalizing *V* leading to his...

Quit it, Nevada.

Arana knocks on the front door, and I hear her bustling in. I grab my clothes for the day and move into the bathing room, where I attempt to ignore Rakiz's deep voice while he murmurs to Arana.

I'm too nervous to eat, but I take a plate and sit in my usual spot. Arana will fuss if she notices I don't have much of an appetite.

Within moments we're left alone, and I shift restlessly, aware of Rakiz's eyes on me.

"Is something wrong?"

I want to ask him one more time, beg him to see reason. But I know he's not going to see things my way. He *can't*.

When I first got here, I was even angrier than I am now. I confronted him when I realized his men had gone to look for our friends without me. His words run through my head now, further cementing my decision.

"The day I allow a female to hunt Voildi is the day I will no longer be fit to rule this tribe. You would die within days. You have no knowledge of this planet and its dangers and no understanding of exactly how much danger you would be in."

He's going to lose his shit when he finds me missing, and what little trust we have between us is going to be smashed to pieces. I wonder who he'll send after me. Rakiz has to assert his authority. He won't be able to help himself.

"Nothing's wrong. I'm just not that hungry." I put down my plate, giving up. "I have to get going."

I pull on my boots and get to my feet, blinking as Rakiz is suddenly standing in front of me.

"Tell me what's wrong. Did someone upset you?"

"No," I choke out, ignoring the lump in my throat, and he frowns, moving closer.

This will be the last time I see him, and I take a moment to memorize his face. It's all hard planes with a nose that has been broken more than once. His lips are the only things that keep him from looking like a brute, and they're full and lush, begging for me to nibble on them.

Fuck it.

I reach out and pull him close, and he doesn't need any further encouragement. His mouth slams down on mine, conquering as his hands slide to my butt, hauling me up until my legs are wrapped around his waist.

I gasp into his mouth, and he responds with a growl, his tongue battling with mine.

God, he's a good kisser.

His hand slides into my hair, angling my head so he can plunder deeper until I'm writhing against him, grinding on his hard, thick—

"Ahem."

I tense. *Oh no.*

"Oh my God," I mumble against Rakiz's mouth, and he ignores me, teeth teasing my bottom lip as the hand on my butt pulls me closer, his cock rubbing against my clit.

"Ahem."

I jolt, using two hands to push against Rakiz's chest until he pulls away. He stares into my eyes for a long moment, cheekbones flushed with arousal, and my eyes drop to his mouth again. I want nothing more than to—

"Nevada." Arana's voice is amused. "There's someone here to see you."

I shove against Rakiz's chest again. "Put me down," I hiss, and he finally complies, although he doesn't let me go —likely using my body to hide his giant erection.

I pinch him, but he holds me tight.

I clear my throat. "I'll be right out, Arana. Thank you."

She smiles at me, her gaze pleased as it flicks from me to Rakiz and back again. Then she nods and turns, moving back into the other room.

Rakiz finally releases me, and I dart away. I avoid his eyes, unwilling to see his satisfaction—or worse, smug triumph.

"Nevada."

I turn, raising my eyes to his. There's none of that on his face. Instead, he looks like a man barely holding onto control. A man with one hell of a raging hard-on.

"We will talk about this," he says.

"Later." The lie is bitter on my tongue. "I need to go. We'll talk later."

His gaze examines my face, looking for...I don't know what. Then he nods, turning and striding out the door.

I watch him leave, strangely sad.

Goodbye, Rakiz.

Nevada

The person at the door is the seamstress's daughter. Her mother sent her with a long, warm cloak for me. I smile, rubbing the thick material.

Clothes. Check.

Now it's time to handle the food. I've already made my arrangements, and I stroll right into the giant food kradi. Several people nod at me in greeting, the servants busy preparing the morning meal.

I hang around, listening to the gossip, and most people ignore me. Finally the moment comes when the kradi is empty for a few scant seconds as people carry meals outside.

Byni—one of the Braxian women—nudges a huge cloth sack at me.

"If you get caught, I had nothing to do with this," she warns, and I nod.

"Thank you."

I haul ass out of the kradi and head to Vivian's. She's nowhere to be found, but I stash the provisions under Alexis's furs, ready to grab later.

Food. Check.

Next I need weapons. I already have my sword, which is always on hand. But at the very least, I'm going to need a couple of good knives. Unfortunately, Rakiz has ensured that every person in this camp knows I'm not allowed anywhere near the kradi where most of the weapons are stashed.

I find Ellie watching Terex train. The warriors aren't using swords right now, and she and I both stand for a moment, enjoying the sight of them engaging in a good, old-fashioned brawl.

Terex takes a vicious kick to the gut, and Ellie flinches beside me. I smirk at her reaction, and we both grin as he leans forward with a brutal right hook, and his opponent goes down.

"I'm ready," I murmur to Ellie, glancing around. I know damn well that Rakiz has eyes on me, and if I'm not where I usually am around this time, someone is sure to narc on me.

"Are you sure I can't talk you out of this?" Ellie's voice is hopeful, but her expression is resigned as she turns to me.

I shake my head. "We need to go now."

She nods and follows me, glancing once more at Terex. We split up, and I take the long way to the weapons kradi, walking quickly but not rushing. The last thing I need is to draw attention.

I position myself behind the kradi and listen in as Ellie gets to work.

"Oh, hey, Braz. Terex has been looking for you. He wants to talk to you."

"He wants to talk to me?" The warrior's voice cracks slightly on the last word, and I grin. Guarding the weapons all day must be boring as hell, and he's likely more than a little excited at the idea of being called by the great Terex himself.

I feel bad. Terex and Rakiz are going to rip him a new one when they find out he left the kradi. It's probably a good lesson to learn. The last thing a guard should be doing is abandoning their post. Ever.

Granted, none of the warriors will be expecting a woman to deceive them. None of the females here would dare.

I roll my eyes at that, but I still feel bad for Ellie. When Terex finds out that she helped me—and he inevitably will —he's going to be livid.

I shrug. Chicks before dick.

"Nevada!"

I've missed the end of the conversation, and Ellie is hissing at me. I creep forward and raise an eyebrow at her expression. She's wide-eyed and pale, glancing around as if expecting to be caught any minute.

"You look guilty as hell. Just stand here and keep an eye out for a moment. Quit looking around. Pretend to be Vivian and examine your nails or something."

She glares at me but takes my advice. I hold back a laugh as she hunches over in front of the weapons kradi, every ounce of her attention on her fingernails.

If someone notices that the guard has left, her bad acting isn't going to fool them for long.

I glance up to the sky.

Give me a hand here, Jack. This shit will be a whole lot easier if you're by my side.

I dart into the kradi, eyes widening as I take in the goodies laid out in front of me. They're stored neatly on shelves, and I'd love nothing more than to spend a few hours in here, examining the medieval-looking swords, knives, and other weapons. I move deeper within the tent and narrow my eyes as I find the knives. They range from tiny throwing knives the length of my little finger to huge hunting knives the length of my arm. I grab a couple—one for fighting up close and one for anything else I might need while out in the wild.

I elbow Ellie as I move past her, and she glances at me, nibbling on her lower lip.

"I wish I could give you a hug," she whispers, and I smile at her.

"Same. I'll be fine, I promise."

Ellie doesn't point out that I have no business promising such a thing on this planet, but she nods. "Be careful."

"I will. I have to go before I lose my window. Don't forget to grab the clothes and food from Vivian's kradi and stash them behind the mishua pen in our spot."

She nods again, her eyes filling with tears, and I wish I could throw my arms around her, but we can't be seen saying goodbye.

"Get out of here before the guard comes back," I say, turning and stalking away.

Weapons. Check.

The next part is the hardest part of my plan and the only part that's completely out of my control. I have to rely on a certain pain in my ass, and my entire plan hinges on her. All I can do is hope that by endlessly drawing Racia's attention to all the other mishua every time they left the pen, I've made my point clear.

She wants freedom? I'm the girl to give it to her.

I strut into the mishua pen, eyeing the warrior guarding it as he nods at me.

"You're late."

"I was talking to Terex. He wants to see you, by the way." I keep my voice nonchalant, striding toward my shovel.

"He wants to see...me?"

I grin. This guy has been an asshole to me ever since I arrived. He seems to feel personally offended every time he sees me wearing my pants, and he's made it clear that if it were up to him, I would be forced to wear a dress and choose a mate.

Unlike with the guard at the weapons kradi, I have zero remorse for how much trouble this guy will be in for abandoning his post.

I shrug as if I couldn't care less. "You're Lariz, right?"

I glance at him out the corner of my eye, picking up my shovel as I move toward my poop mountain.

He doesn't even look back at me. He's too busy heading toward the training arena.

Idiot.

I eye the mishua, who bares her teeth at me, likely picking up on my anxiety. I force myself to take a deep breath and then blow it out.

"Here's the thing. You want out; I want out. You have approximately ten seconds to decide if you want your freedom. Otherwise, I'm taking one of the other mishua."

She stares at me, and I shrug, moving toward the herd, which gathers on the opposite side of the pen. I'm bluffing, of course. None of the other mishua will allow me near them.

Racia snorts, and I hide my grin as she comes up behind me.

"No funny business, then," I tell her. I glance around and then climb over the pen, grab the bags Ellie hid for me, and climb back inside, where Racia stares at me with her red eyes.

"Yep, you have to carry me *and* my stuff. I know for whatever reason you're not a fan of women, but would you rather have a short exercise ride with a warrior or an adventure with me?"

I let her think about it while I grab her saddle from the attached kradi, which passes as a tack room. I've never actually saddled one of these beasts, but you bet your ass I watched closely every single time someone did it in my presence.

I turn with the saddle in my arms, and the mishua waits.

"I'm choosing to take this as a sign that you're all in," I mutter.

I move closer, ready to leap out of the way if she decides to kill me, but she stays still, allowing me to saddle her up.

I attach the bags to the saddle, and my breath comes faster. I don't have long now. If I get caught…

I push that thought away. The last thing I need to do is make this mishua even more skittish.

I take the cloak from one of the bags and pull the hood over my head. Then I pick up a handful of dirt and smear it on Racia's skin.

She lets out a growl, whipping her head toward me, and I duck, barely avoiding being gored.

"Don't be an asshole." My hands are shaking at the close call. "Look, dummy. All the other mishua are dark green all over. You've got those lighter patches right there on either side. Probably why Rakiz chose you, the vain idiot. If we don't cover them up, the sentries are going to notice that you're the king's mishua, and we're both screwed."

I move toward her again, and she shies away. Frustration hits me, and to my shock, useless tears almost rise to my eyes.

This is my only shot at finding the other women. If I'm caught now, Rakiz will never let me out of his sight again.

I turn away, attempting to get ahold of myself. Then I jump back as the mishua snorts into my ear.

"For fuck's sake, are you trying to give me a heart attack?"

She stands as if she doesn't have a care in the world, eyeing me like she's wondering what I'm upset about. I freeze as she slowly moves toward me, shoving her head under my hand, which is still filled with mud.

"Are you sure? 'Cause I don't have time for temper tantrums. Fuck me around again, and I'm taking one of the others."

It's an empty threat, and I suspect she knows it, but I sigh, slowly raising my hand toward the lime-green scales on her side.

"These are beautiful," I murmur. "It's a shame to cover them up."

She tosses her head, and I'm pretty sure she's preening. I laugh, and then I jump into action, stepping around her and swiping the mud down her other side until those scales are covered.

It's now or never.

I want to lead her to the fence and use it as a mounting block, but if I can't get on her now, there's no way I'll be able to do it out in the wild.

I'm not graceful, but I manage to haul myself up onto the mishua's back, my muscles straining. Racia stands still, although her muscles are more tense than I've ever seen them. I adjust my cloak so that it covers me completely, making sure my hair is tucked underneath.

"Right, let's get the hell out of here."

While the odds are against me with this escape attempt, I have a few things going for me as well. For one, no one is going to expect me to ride out of here on a mishua. After all, the beasts are often challenging for even the most experienced warriors.

I push that thought down. If I think about all the ways I can end up dead in a ditch somewhere, I'll go curl up in Rakiz's furs and never leave his hut again.

My chest hurts at the thought of the tribe king. My experience staying with him has taught me that beneath the arrogance and high-handedness, Rakiz is just a man. A man who is going to lose his shit when he finds me gone.

That thought gets me moving even more than the thought of the guard coming back, and I knee the mishua.

While I sat on Leai's back on my way to camp that first day, I wasn't at all in control of where she walked. Asroz had tied her to his mishua, and all I had to do was sit and contemplate how I could find the other women.

Now I need to steer her myself.

It's not completely dissimilar to riding a horse, except that a horse is unlikely to throw you and gore you with huge horns if it feels you've been disrespectful.

"Come on, Racia. We need to get out of here before the guard comes back."

She either understands or senses my urgency because she speeds up. I grit my teeth, holding on tightly. I'm not sure if the Braxians picked mishua to tame and ride because of their fearlessness in battle or because they're the only option on this planet. But they sure didn't pick them for their smooth ride.

I'm covered with sweat under my cloak as we leave the camp, passing a group of sentries. They're busy ribbing one another, talking about their last battle with the Voildi.

I grimace. Rakiz should thank me for this. At the very least, I've exposed the numerous holes and flaws in his security. If someone as well known and distinctive looking as me can get *out*, then who else could find a way to sneak *in*?

I shiver at the thought but turn my attention to the horizon, patting the map I've tucked away under my cloak. I'll head west until I'm far enough away from the camp to stop and check my map, and then I'll adjust as necessary.

"Hold on, you guys. I'm coming for you."

CHAPTER FIVE

R *akiz*

I STALK THROUGH MY CAMP, SHAKING WITH FURY.

For once, my name isn't called, and people don't follow in my wake, needing my attention. Today they jump out of the way, faces paling.

Nevada is nowhere to be seen.

I would not necessarily expect to see her throughout the day, although I usually manage to at least watch some of her training with Asroz. Today, though, one of the males who tends to the mishua mentioned that he often sees her when he comes to feed the mishua, and today she wasn't there.

The female is stubborn, but she is never late. I nodded, trying to ignore the way my stomach twisted, well aware that no one would dare touch Nevada within my camp.

Unfortunately, one of the warriors found a servant crying behind the food kradi. When he asked why, she admitted to providing Nevada with food for her *journey*.

The journey that began when she stole my mishua. The mishua that no one noticed missing until right now, which means that Nevada has been gone for *hours*.

I stride into Terex's tent, and he growls as he pushes his female behind him.

"Where is she?" I roar, ignoring the spark of guilt as the small female cowers. Nevada would roar back at me, and the thought of her alone and in danger darkens my mood further.

Terex steps into my space, attempting to cover Ellie's body with his. "Rakiz," he says, keeping his voice even, "what is this?"

I ignore him. "Tell me, female," I say, and her chin juts out stubbornly.

The sight enrages me. Panic is twisting my insides into knots. The sooner I understand where she is going, the sooner I can find her.

"Watch yourself, Rakiz," Terex says, stepping closer, and I stare him down.

"The hellion has disappeared. I don't believe she acted alone." In fact, I know it. All this time, I was fooling myself believing that no one would betray me, that my wishes would be respected—if not by Nevada, then by my people.

"Is this true?" Terex asks Ellie.

"I—" she starts.

I don't have time for this. "Where did she go?" I growl.

"Where do you think?" The female's voice is shaking, but she manages to hold my gaze. "She went looking for our friends."

I curse. I know that much. "Where?"

"I don't know. She's been listening in and making plans. She figured out where they're most likely to be taken."

I turn to Terex, more furious than I've ever been in my life. "She took my mishua."

Ellie covers her face while Terex stares at me in stunned silence.

"How could she have taken it?"

My jaw aches from grinding my teeth. "I had her working in the mishua pen. She likely took the opportunity to build some sort of relationship with the beast."

I had noticed her talking to the mishua and I found the habit cute.

Cute.

Ellie's voice is timid. "If the mishua allowed her to ride it, it can't be that dangerous, right?"

I turn away, unable to speak, and Terex sighs.

"The mishua may allow her to ride it one moment and then kill her the next," he says. "The king's mishua is highly intelligent and easily bored. It may allow Nevada on its back purely for the chance to return to the wild."

I can't listen anymore. "I will find her," I snarl, stalking from the kradi.

I go straight to the other female's kradi, walking in and ignoring Vivian's squeak.

"Where did she go?"

"I don't know—"

"*Where?*" I roar, and she pales even as her jaw firms. These human females are stubborn and loyal but none more so than Nevada.

The thought of her on my mishua, currently traveling further and further from safety...

I step forward, and Vivian's eyes widen.

"Sh-She made a map," she says. "She took it with her."

"Which direction is she heading?"

She stares at me, and I force myself to soften my tone.

"She will die if you don't tell me where she's going, female. I can prevent her death."

Her eyes fill with tears. "Back toward where we were found. I think she wanted to retrace our steps and look for any tracks. But she also mentioned the Seinex Forest and Nexia."

Oh gods.

Vivian chokes out a sob, and I turn, heading straight back to my tashiv, where Arana is waiting for me, her face pale.

"Did you know?" I ask.

"No." She shakes her head. "I swear. When I saw you two this morning...I thought Nevada had given up her plans to leave."

I clench my fists, betrayal stabbing through me.

The best kiss of my life, and for her it was a goodbye.

Nevada

I have a lot of time to think out here alone. The sun beats down overhead, and I pull off my cloak once I'm far enough from the camp that I'm unlikely to be spotted.

The nights are still cool here, requiring a fire. But the days are beginning to warm up.

This isn't the first time I've run away. When I was a teenager, I was always playing truant. School bored me. I was smart enough to pass whatever tests I had to take whenever I was actually *at* school. But staying in school was a problem when I knew my time could be better spent doing odd jobs for a few dollars.

I was the youngest. My brother had split when I was

twelve, and I couldn't blame him really. It would've been nice if he'd called once or twice, but I think the guilt got to him. He knew he was leaving me to deal with our mother alone.

In his mind, it was probably my turn to handle it anyway given how many times he'd rolled her onto her side so she wouldn't choke on her own puke. He tried his best to shelter me from the realities of living with an alcoholic parent.

We never knew our father. Given how different we looked and the seven-year age gap between us, it's unlikely that we even had the same father.

I was a smart kid, and I found ways to steal food and money. During the few hours a week when my mother was sober, I could usually convince her to hand over a few dollars of her unemployment check so I could buy the bare minimum—often a loaf of white bread and some peanut butter.

"Hold on, Racia. I need to look at the map."

She ignores me until I pull on the thin strap that passes for reins. The idea of mishua taking bits in their mouths is laughable, so the reins are wrapped around their snouts, and Racia seems to treat all my pulls and tugs as merely suggestions.

Racia snorts but finally stops, and I wait a moment. I wouldn't be surprised if she decides to take off now that I've relaxed—if only so she can watch as I hit the ground.

She seems like she isn't necessarily planning to go anywhere, so I pull out my map, examining my crude sketch.

Unfortunately, thanks to my limited knowledge of this planet and the difficult materials I'm working with, it kind of looks like a five-year-old drew a map of their backyard. At least I have a rough idea of where I'm going. We need to travel north, through the Seinex Forest and back toward the clearing where the Braxians fought with the Voildi.

We all learned how to read maps in the military, but I never could've imagined that I'd be using those skills on an alien planet.

When I was a kid, I knew there was only one way out of poverty. College wasn't in my future unless I could one day go on the G.I. Bill. The moment I turned seventeen, I convinced my mother to provide parental consent and went down to the local recruitment office.

In the marines, I found people just like me. People from all sorts of backgrounds. Some of them wanted to serve their country. Others just wanted a steady income and to get out of whatever situation they'd found themselves in.

Most of us found what we were looking for.

I make it to the edge of the forest as night falls. Ellie once described it as a "horror movie" forest, and I can see why. The trees are all bone white, reflecting the light as the sun goes down. Their branches are long and thin, stretching downward as if waiting to grab me as I move past them.

Traveling through this forest at night? That's a nope from me. If I sleep now and get up at first light, I'll be in the clearing and searching before the day gets too hot.

I slide off the mishua and tie her to one of the trees at the edge of the forest. The ground is hard here, and the night is cold enough that I'm going to have to light a fire, which is a risk that could draw predators close. Something tells me that I'm not going to get much sleep tonight.

"Ow." My feet hit the ground, and I grit my teeth at the pain. Just a few hours of riding, and every muscle hurts, including my neck and shoulders—likely from the tension I've been holding all day.

I groan and mutter some more while I set up my camp. I

have enough water in my skins to last me the night, but I'll have to find more as soon as I'm up and moving in the morning.

I feed Racia and then curl up on the hard ground, teeth chattering as it gets colder. I wish I had a thicker blanket now, and I'd give just about anything for one of the furs I crawled under each night in Rakiz's tashiv.

I don't sleep. At one point, I almost snooze, but then a noise nearby makes me jump and clutch my knife in my hand, barely breathing.

When morning comes, I'm exhausted but still alive, so I count it as a win. As soon as I can see my hand in front of my face, I pack up my tent and throw the saddle on the mishua.

I manage to make it back to the clearing. If there's one thing I'm good at, it's directions, and I took care to memorize as much as I could when we were led from the ship. I tie Racia to a tree and then comb over every inch of the clearing and the surrounding area.

I sigh, frustrated, and head back to where I tied the mishua. I'm thirsty, and I can't risk getting dehydrated. I spotted a small stream about a hundred feet away, so I lead the mishua back with me and tie her to another tree where I can keep an eye on her.

The water looks fresh enough to drink, but I don't risk it. You never know when there's a dead animal lying a few hundred feet away in the same water.

The Braxians have a specific type of rock that they use to purify water. I have no idea what it's made out of, but thankfully Byni tucked a few in with my food. I didn't even think of doing the same, and I'm glad I don't have to risk lighting a fire.

Once I've drunk my fill and collected water for later, I

eye the stream. It's about twenty feet wide, but it looks shallow enough that the water would probably only come up to my midthigh.

I frown. The Braxians can smell the Voildi, and they say they stink. But what if they walked back and crossed the stream, waiting for us to leave the area before choosing a new direction?

"We need to go across the stream."

Racia eyes it, letting out a loud snort, and I sigh as I scrabble my way back up onto her back.

"What now? You're afraid of a little water?"

She snorts again, obviously offended, but doesn't move.

"If you make me cross that river alone, I'm going to tell all the other mishua back at the camp when we return. You'll be a coward. A laughingstock. No one will respect you anymore."

I yelp, almost losing my seat as the mishua throws her head. Her gaze is dark red with fury as she turns her head, staring me in the eye.

I wouldn't be at all surprised if she started breathing fire.

"It's true," I say, somehow preventing my voice from shaking. "Come on, Racia. What's a little water?"

She trembles, her head lowering, sharp horns glinting at me in the sun. Somehow, I *know* that she'd like nothing more than to pierce me with those horns and throw me off her back to choke on my own blood.

Finally—finally—she turns, slowly walking toward the stream. She picks up her feet, and I choke on a laugh as she *prances* like a show pony, slowly moving through the water and then rushing up the bank on the other side. I curse as I nearly fall, but I give her a pat as we make it up the small hill.

"Oh my God."

On the ground six feet in front of me, half buried in the dirt and standing out like a flag...a scrap of pink material that looks suspiciously like Ivy's Minnie Mouse pajamas.

I slide off the mishua, my entire focus on the material. Ivy seemed smart and capable when we first met, and I mentally high-five her as I pick up the pink cotton. Ivy's counting on all of them, and she was resourceful enough to leave us a clue for when we came looking.

My hands shake, and I swallow down bile. Rakiz's men obviously didn't cross the stream. They're so used to following their noses that they didn't expect the Voildi to outsmart them. If Rakiz had let me go with his men when I first asked, we'd be so much closer to finding them.

Despair and determination battle within me, and I grind my teeth. I'm here now. If Ivy's left one clue behind, she'll have left more. I just need to find them.

I glance at the mishua, who seems strangely calm. I move closer, and she sniffs at my hair as I tie her to another tree.

"You stay here for a few minutes. I'm going to search this area and figure out which direction they would've traveled in."

Racia ignores me, and then she jerks her head up, almost impaling me with one of her horns. I scowl at her, and then my breath leaves my lungs in a rush.

Someone is coming.

CHAPTER SIX

N*evada*

A BRANCH CRACKS, AND I FREEZE.

Oh shit.

I whirl, and my heart leaps into my throat as I meet Rakiz's dark eyes.

How the hell did he find me?

He rushes me, and I jolt, completely unprepared for the movement.

I sidestep, but he's on me, and he blocks my right hook as I swing, so I follow it up with a knee to the gut.

Oof. That hurt my knee, so it must've hurt his abdomen, right?

He simply steps to the side as if my knee never connected. Great.

Rakiz's eyes narrow dangerously, and I bare my teeth in a feral grin. For such a huge guy, he's fucking fast, and I'm mentally thanking Asroz for my fancy footwork as I dart away, dodging his attempt to grab me.

I bat his hand away. "What the hell are you doing here? You can't leave the camp!"

"Strange, you took the words out of my mouth." Rakiz glowers at me and then glances over my shoulder, eyes widening slightly. I turn my head to see his mishua watching us intently.

Then I'm cursing as Rakiz lunges forward, taking advantage of my inattention and batting my punch away as if my arm is a particularly annoying insect.

I trip him, but he takes me down with him—twisting so I land on top of him as he prevents me from hitting the ground.

Those protective instincts cost him, and I have my knife out and nestled against his throat when we land.

He ignores it, rolling his body until I'm trapped under him. He surrounds me on all sides, leaning down until his face is inches from mine, my knife still pressed against his skin.

I narrow my eyes at him. "Why did you follow me?"

"You know why."

"I'm not going back."

"You'll do as I say."

I snarl, and his eyes drop to my mouth before his gaze returns to mine.

Suddenly, his face is no longer furious, and I can feel him hard and thick against me.

"Um...your point is made. You can let me up."

"I don't think so."

I blow out a frustrated breath. I can't deny the fact that it's nice to see him. But it'd be a lot nicer if he wasn't here to drag me back to his camp.

"You disobeyed me."

I sigh. Some people are surprised to learn that I have issues with authority. After all I'm a marine, and I'm used to taking orders...right?

Wrong.

"Once again, you're not in charge of me."

"You'll soon learn otherwise."

I open my mouth to give him a piece of my mind, and he obviously sees the move as an invitation because his mouth is suddenly there, his lips caressing mine as his hard body shelters me protectively.

Kissing him is like riding the biggest roller coaster at my favorite theme park...twice.

Rakiz seduces my mouth, and I open further, my body relaxing under his as my brain turns off, and all that matters are the electric charges sparking around my body.

He moves back, and I stare at him, stunned. My head feels dizzy and my body fevered, and all I want to do is drag him closer even as my brain turns back on.

He leans forward, and I slap my hand over his mouth. "No. Get off me."

He stares at me for a long moment, and then I feel him grin against my hand as he rolls off my body, getting to his feet without using his hands. "I scare you."

"Don't be ridiculous."

"You want me, and it scares you. Good to know. Get on my mishua. We're leaving."

"I'm not going anywhere."

He ignores that, walking toward Racia. A snort leaves him as he takes in the dirt I smeared on either side of her body. I glance around. He must have brought another mishua with him. Maybe while he's distracted, I can—

"Don't even think about it."

I scowl at his back, and he turns, raising one eyebrow as he gestures for me to come closer.

I hold up my hand and give him a gesture of my own, and he narrows his eyes.

"I am bigger than you and stronger than you. I can haul you back to camp tied like a prisoner. Don't. Push. Me."

My scowl deepens at the reminder of how much bigger he is than me. He knows just how to push all my buttons.

I hold up the material in my hand, and his dark gaze follows it.

"You know what this is?"

"What?"

"It's a piece of material that Ivy managed to rip off her pajamas. Granted, they were basically rags anyway, but the point remains. The other women didn't go the way you thought they did. Your warriors have been searching the wrong area."

His gaze shifts from the scrap of material back to my face. He's silent for a long moment, and I seize my chance.

"Look, Rakiz, I don't deny that your warriors are strong and fearsome. I'm sure they could find the other women *if they knew where they were.* But this just proves that they don't."

He nods. "I will send more warriors to this spot."

I grind my teeth. "We'll just lose more time."

"We can check the surrounding area while we're here."

I hate the way he says it, like he's doing *me* a favor by *allowing* me to search. But I nod anyway, turning around as I look for any sign of the women passing through here.

"They would've been struggling," I say. I curse as I scan our surroundings. If I made my way back here sooner, maybe there would have been some fresh tracks to follow.

"The Voildi will have had to carry them the whole way,

which would've slowed them down and made any tracks deeper," I continue.

Rakiz nods and moves toward me, pointing toward the east. "Look," he says, and I step forward.

It's not much, just a rock that's been overturned. But it's darker on the exposed side, and I can see the impression where it used to rest.

I nod. "Okay, they came up the hill and waited until we were gone. Then they went that way."

I move toward the rock, and Rakiz catches my arm. I whirl impatiently.

"What are you doing?" he asks.

"What does it look like I'm doing? I'm following the obvious tracks that your men missed."

Rakiz shakes his head, and I pull my arm out of his grip. I hate that I only succeed because he lets me go.

"If you take me back to that camp, I will hate you. I will never stop trying to escape, and I will never forgive you for preventing me from helping my friends. Do you understand?"

Rakiz looks at me thoughtfully for a long moment.

"I'm beginning to." He sighs, running a hand over his face. For the first time since I've known him, he looks tired. "Perhaps we can bargain."

I sigh. Ellie told me all about Terex's "bargains," and obviously Rakiz is cut from the same cloth.

"What?"

"Once at least one of these women are found, you will swear on your honor that you will not leave camp again without my permission. And you won't be allowed out of my sight until I feel I can trust you."

I grind my teeth. "You're a real dick sometimes, you know that?"

He simply waits me out.

I tilt my head. "You don't think Beth, Ivy, and Zoey will be together?"

He shrugs. "Like you, I hope this is so. But we don't know if they have been separated. If I had the women, I would send each to a different area within my territory in case we were attacked."

I eye him. I'm guessing that statements like that are why he's known as such a good ruler. He's always considering the angles.

"If I find one or more of them and they know where the others are, we'll go after them and then return to camp. If they don't, we'll come back, and you can send warriors after them. Deal?"

"Fine. You may look for the other females."

Relief steals my breath, and I tilt my head at him. "Seriously?"

He nods.

"Okay, then. Well, I'll see you when I'm back at camp."

"You misunderstand. I'm not leaving you."

I glower at him and then turn away and kick a rock, watching it roll down the small hill. It's always something with this guy. "Look, Rakiz."

"Don't even try it."

"Are you even allowed to be away from the camp? Do your babysitters know where you are?"

A muscle ticks in his jaw at my question, and I hold back a grin. His council members will be losing their minds.

I admire his control as he lets out a breath, his eyes narrowing on me. Yep, I know how to push his buttons too.

"I am the king," he says softly. "I'm allowing this foolishness even though we are hopelessly outnumbered in the event that we come across any Voildi. Do not make me regret it."

"Look, you should go back and send more warriors here. We may need backup."

"And leave you alone? No."

I sigh. Is it a dumb move for the tribe king to come with me? Sure. But I need to find my friends. "It's on your head."

He just sends me a patronizing look and gestures toward the rock. I roll my eyes but move forward.

There's a narrow path between the trees, and I glance back at the mishua. If we travel single file, we can make it. "Let's follow it for a little bit and then come back for the mishua."

Rakiz nods, and I step between the trees. I shiver, still creeped out by their long white branches. I wouldn't be at all surprised if they suddenly whipped out, wrapping around my waist and pulling me—

"Are you okay?"

I glance back at Rakiz, raising my eyebrows.

"You're breathing faster."

"Stay focused, big guy."

Around ten minutes later, the trees clear slightly, and we can go either left or right. The Voildi were either arrogant enough to think we wouldn't track them or they didn't have time to cover up their tracks.

My guess? It's a bit of both. I note a broken branch that leads us to the right, and we move silently until we get to another fork. One path crosses over another stream, and the other leads deeper into the trees.

I grin. "Ivy, you genius." She's left another scrap of material, like a tiny pink flag, stuck between the branches of one of the trees.

Rakiz examines it. "How did the Voildi not notice?"

"My guess? They would've carried the women over their shoulders. If Ivy was at the back, she could've reached up as she went past."

In my mind's eye, I can see her desperately slapping out her hand, hoping to God that the scrap of cotton won't be blown away or used as part of a nest by an enterprising bird.

"It just brings it home, you know? How much they're depending on us." I turn to Rakiz, who studies me with dark eyes. "Let's get the mishua," I say. "They went across the stream."

Rakiz

Nevada is not pleased when I order her onto the mishua I rode here and tie the beast to Racia.

"You know I rode the mishua perfectly well by myself on the way here, right?"

"Yes, and the fact that I found you alive will surprise me until the day I die."

"You're such a drama king. Me and Racia are like this." Nevada holds up her hand, one finger crossed over the other, and Racia snorts.

"Regardless, it's not happening now. Get on the mishua."

She rolls her eyes but doesn't argue, desperate to get to her friends.

Guilt hits me again. If my warriors had been better prepared, perhaps they would have found the females before now. As their king, their failure is my failure. If the females are dead or injured...the fault lies with me.

I watch as Nevada hauls herself onto the mishua. She is incredibly strong for her size, and I almost groan as I imagine tumbling her. All that strength and stamina, that smart mouth and those emerald eyes—

"Are you ready to go or what?"

Nevada eyes me, almost as if she knows exactly where my mind was. My gaze drops to her mouth, but I turn the mishua, and we head back the way we came.

Once we reach the stream, we can travel side by side, and I wait until Nevada pulls forward.

"What's this mishua's name?"

"Kazi."

Nevada smiles, and I have to look away. When we are together, this female is all scowls and frowns, glowers and eye rolls. Oh, I've seen her laughing when I've caught her with her friends or watched her training with Asroz. My mood turns dark at the thought of the warrior training Nevada, but I push it away.

I am glad this female doesn't know the power of her smile. If she were to smile up at me...I would likely give her anything she wanted.

I frown at the thought, and Nevada glances at me as we make our way out of the water. There is only one path between the trees, and we follow it, looking for signs of the human females.

It has been a long time since I've been in the wilderness like this without being surrounded by guards. Here, I can hear myself think. I can enjoy the fresh air. I can pretend that I'm just a male enjoying a ride with a beautiful female.

I frown. "There," I say, pointing.

Nevada narrows her eyes. "They took the time to leave decoys, hoping we'd go in circles. They obviously figured they had more time once they got this far away."

I nod. They couldn't have completely erased their tracks

while carrying three human females. So they've attempted to lead anyone who tracks them in circles.

Nevada opens her mouth, and I glare at her.

"No."

"You don't even know what I—"

"You want to separate. No."

Surprisingly, she doesn't argue, although I can hear her muttering as we head to the left.

"Bossy bastard," she says, and I can't help but grin.

"Tracks," I say, and she jumps off the mishua.

I dismount as well. "What are you doing?"

"Suddenly there are tracks while there were none before? I don't believe it for a second." She crouches, angling her head. "Yeah, look. They had to press deep for the footprints to last this long. And look at the way the soil scatters here. They walked backwards. Do they think we're idiots?"

I sigh. "For Braxians, Voildi stink. We are used to simply following our noses. Usually that is all we need to do to find any packs we are hunting. But this pack is smarter and more organized than any we have hunted before. My warriors would not have been expecting this type of thinking from them."

Nevada nods and pulls herself back onto the mishua. "Makes sense."

Her tone has no blame, but I think about this situation on the way back to the right path. The intelligent human female—Ivy, I remember—was unable to leave any trace of the direction of their travel at this point.

"Yeah," Nevada says when I voice my thoughts. "I'm hoping that it was just because their order of travel was changed and maybe she couldn't risk it without them figuring out what she was doing."

Neither of us mention the other possibility—that she was unconscious or her hands were tied and we will have to focus solely on reading the Voildi tracks.

I clear my throat, and Nevada glances at me.

"When we return to camp," I say, ignoring her frown at my words, "would you consider teaching some of my warriors about tracking without relying on their noses?"

She tilts her head, but the ghost of a smile plays around her lips. "Really?"

I nod. "Of course. This is a skill you are excellent at. This trip proves that this pack of Voildi can outmaneuver my warriors. If one pack can do this, it is only a matter of time before they can all do it."

Nevada grins at me, and her smile drops as I stare. She turns her attention back to the forest.

"What?" she mutters.

"You are a beautiful female."

She snorts as if she doesn't believe me, and I frown, opening my mouth, but then she points.

"Check that out."

I examine the tiny pink cloth, which has been shoved inside a fallen log.

"They got tired." Nevada's voice is triumphant. "And they dumped the women on the ground. Idiots. Look at all these tracks. I can just imagine Ivy sitting here, pushing that material in that log. And look—one of the other women sat here and ripped up a handful of grass."

Nevada glances at me, face hard, eyes shining with determination. "They're fighters, all of them. They must have been terrified, but they knew we'd come for them." She smiles. "You know, we'd only known each other a couple of days. But they knew we wouldn't leave them behind."

"I'm sorry," I say, and Nevada's gaze meets mine. "I failed

you and the other females. I should have listened and should have allowed you to return."

Nevada looks at me for a long moment, and then she nods, the corner of her mouth kicking up, and I want nothing more than to pull her close and kiss her again.

"It's okay," she says, turning back to the log. "You're here now."

CHAPTER SEVEN

N*evada*

We travel all day, but eventually it's too dark to see the path in front of us.

Rakiz scans our surroundings as we set up camp. I'm feeding the mishua while he pulls a piece of material similar to canvas out of one of his packs.

"We cannot afford to light a fire this deep in the forest," he says, and I nod. It'll be cold, but it's not like it's going to snow.

We refilled our waterskins earlier, and I turn to gulp at some water before pulling out my rations.

Rakiz stares at me for a moment and then reaches into his own bag. My mouth waters at the sight of the sweet cakes I love. I have a huge sweet tooth, and Rakiz's sudden grin tells me he knows it.

I scowl at him. That smile should be illegal.

His grin widens. "Tell me how you snuck out of my camp, and I will give you a sweet cake."

"Are you kidding me? That's worth at least three sweet cakes."

He laughs, and I stare, mesmerized. Since we've been away from camp, it's like a weight has fallen off Rakiz's shoulders. Even though we spent all day working to find the women, his brow is no longer constantly creased in a frown. His eyes are quicker to light with amusement, and he's the most relaxed I've ever seen him.

"Two," he bargains. "And one in the morning."

"I can live with that. But...no one who helped me can get into any trouble."

Rakiz's face hardens. "They disobeyed me."

"They did it because they either understood why I needed to go, they saw me as a threat to you—and therefore, the camp—or they were just naive and easily manipulated." I leave out the seamstress, who just wanted me gone so her daughter could flirt with Rakiz.

He studies my face, and a muscle ticks in his jaw as he nods.

"Okay." I sigh. "First...your warriors were the easiest to trick."

Rakiz narrows his eyes at me, and I throw up my hands.

"You wanted the truth! It's like with the Voildi. None of them have been smart enough to cover their tracks before, so your men didn't expect it. The same thing happened at camp. No woman had ever lied to their faces the way I did, so they didn't expect it. Tell me, if another warrior had come up to Lariz and told him that Terex wanted to see him *right at that moment*, would he have left his post?"

Rakiz turns his head, staring into the distance, and I give him a moment to think, ripping into the dried meat I brought with me. I offer him the cloth bag, and he takes a few pieces. Both of us munch until he returns his attention to me.

"I do not believe he would have."

I nod. "The same thing happened with the weapons. All I had to do was drop Terex's name, and I was free." Rakiz's face hardens again, and I sigh. "Look, your warriors are well trained; they just need a few reminders. It's a good thing that all I wanted to do was sneak out. What if I'd really been trying to let someone else *in?*"

I grab some more dried meat and grimace at the chewiness. It's protein and calories, both of which I need after such a long day, but the meat is definitely a lot better when fresh.

No one likes to hear that they have massive holes in their security, but to Rakiz's credit, he seems to be taking me seriously. "What do you suggest?"

"Well, your instinct would be to publicly shame the people who let me out, right?"

"*Shame* is a strong word, but they should be punished, yes."

I shake my head. "Wrong tactic to take. All that's going to do is create resentment. Especially against the human women. I can take it, but it's not fair if the others are treated differently."

"So what do you suggest?"

I eye him, but he's truly interested, and I shift on the mishua blanket I'm using to protect my pants from the slightly damp grass.

"Make it a game. Get the Braxian females involved. Keep it a secret at first until all of the guards and sentries have been tested. Then you can reveal that you were testing them. Sure, they'll all be a bit embarrassed at first, but I can guarantee there will be more of them fooled than those who aren't. And then you can give them a wake-up call. Where I come from, if a soldier leaves their post..." I shake my head, and Rakiz leans forward.

"They are punished, aren't they? And yet you're suggesting that those who allowed you to leave the camp shouldn't be punished?"

I sigh. "It's different."

"How?"

"Well, first, it's always going to be easier to get *out* of a camp than to get in, so I had that going for me. Second, I'm sneakier than most." I grin at him, but he leans forward, catching my chin.

His hand tightens as I attempt to yank my head away, so I coolly raise one eyebrow.

"Anything could have happened, Nevada. A pack of Voildi could have torn you to pieces, or that mishua could have thrown you at the first opportunity, leaving you with only that sword and no food or supplies. You seem to think that you're invincible or that your life doesn't matter. Why is this?"

I narrow my eyes at him, pissed off. "You know what I think every time I take a bath or crawl under those warm furs or eat a fucking meal? Those other women may have none of that. We were *all* taken from Earth, and by the luck of the draw, I ended up with you guys and they got taken by those assholes. They're tough, but they've been gone for a while now. Beth's a fucking *ballerina,* for Christ's sake. They should've taken me instead."

I yank my head again, and this time he lets go, so I move away, getting to my feet.

"You don't just get to throw your life away because you feel guilty," he snarls, rising to face me.

He still doesn't get it. "That's not what I was doing. I took an educated risk based on my training and the tools I had available to me. You may think that all women are good for is looking pretty in dresses and birthing babies, but on my planet, we're worth more than that."

He curses, a word that my translator can't seem to find. "Do you truly believe I think that way?"

I throw up my hands. I'm not sure how we got to this point, but obviously I've got a lot to get off my chest. "Why wouldn't I? Time and time again, you've stopped me from doing shit I want to do because I'm a *female*. I understand that some of it's cultural, but you have to see where I'm coming from. I've been to *war*, Rakiz. But because I have breasts, you seem to think that it doesn't matter."

He's silent for a long moment, and then he strides forward, cupping my face in his hands. "I am sorry if I made you feel this way. It is true, I am not used to seeing a female with a sword in her hand. But I do respect you. You have outsmarted my warriors and tracked the Voildi using your superior skills. You are brave and fierce and loyal, and I admire that. But I have a need to keep you safe, Nevada. Never will I allow you to be hurt if I can prevent it."

I blow out a breath, depressed. There's that a-word again. It shouldn't matter. After all, I'm not going to be around here for long anyway. But strangely, it does.

Rakiz's gaze scans my face, his warm hands still cradling my head. "You mean something to me, female. I don't understand it, but I need you to know...it is not because you have breasts." His gaze flicks down and then back up to my face, and this time it holds amusement. "It is because I want you for myself."

My mouth drops open, and Rakiz doesn't hesitate. He leans down and presses his warm lips to mine.

Rakiz

The taste of this female, the feel of her body, the way her mouth softens under mine...

I growl against her lips, wrapping my arm around her waist as I pull her close. I half expect her to push me away, but instead, the tiniest moan escapes her throat, encouraging me further.

She slides the tip of her tongue inside my mouth, licking and playing. She tastes delicious—like the currant fruits she was eating earlier and pure female temptation.

I bury my hand in her hair and hold her right where I want her. This female feels as evanescent as smoke. Like she may just disappear if I don't keep her close. I want to roar as she shivers, and a hum of pleasure leaves her as she slides her hands around my neck.

Then she's slowly pulling away, her emerald eyes a dark green. She bites her lip, looking suddenly vulnerable, and it's this, more than anything, that makes me release her.

"This is a bad idea," she says.

I nod as if in agreement, and she moves back toward the blanket she was sitting on. I take a deep breath and then blow it out, amusement hitting me. I'm suddenly like a young, untested warrior—hard and ready, my body tense with the urge to roll Nevada beneath me. To make her admit that she wants me as much as I want her.

I have never wanted anything as much as I want the prickly, stubborn female who is currently hunching her shoulders as she picks at her rations, carefully ignoring me.

The fact that she can't seem to look at me tells me all I need to know.

She wants me too.

I reach into my pack and then pull out my hand, holding it in front of her. She looks up, and I open my fingers, revealing her sweet cakes. Her eyes light up, and she snatches them away, her hands lightning quick.

Somehow, even while fury raged through my body as I packed for this trip, I remembered to bring treats for the female who ties me in knots.

I care for my mishua and then roll out the thick fur that we will sleep on, Nevada's words running through my mind. While they make me grind my teeth, I can't blame her for her assumption. But how does a warrior protect a female who doesn't *want* to be protected without losing any good feelings she may have for him?

She made her thoughts on this clear earlier. *"If you take me back to that camp, I will hate you. I will never stop trying to escape, and I will never forgive you for preventing me from helping my friends."*

Nevada turns, her gaze focused somewhere over my shoulder. "We should get some sleep so we can be up as soon as we've got some light."

I nod, gesturing to where I've set up our bed. While I have been caring for my mishua, Nevada has done the same with Kazi, and now she stands with a blanket wrapped around her shoulders.

"I'll sleep alone," she says, and I slowly shake my head, holding back a grin.

"It will be too cold for you with just that thin blanket and no fire. We will need to sleep together for warmth." I'm not lying, but I can't deny that the thought of sleeping next to her warm body pleases me. I keep my expression neutral as her eyes scan my face and then I turn away to hide my triumph when she finally nods, her practical nature winning over whatever reservations she may have.

I'm no longer denying it—to either her or myself. I crave Nevada, and when she is ready, I will make her scream my name in pleasure.

Nevada crawls under the furs, and I take off my boots and then do the same. I snort as she turns her back to me, and then I reach out and pull her close, ignoring her curses.

"Body heat, female. Go to sleep."

I can almost *feel* her rolling her eyes, but within a few minutes, her breathing deepens, and she falls asleep in my arms.

⸻

Nevada

I can tell I dreamed last night. I don't remember any of the nightmares, but Rakiz is giving me the same careful look he sometimes did the few times I woke up late and we ate breakfast together in his tashiv.

His eyes scan my face, and I raise one eyebrow even though I want to grit my teeth. I can control the way I react to most things during the day, although this man makes me act impulsive and cranky, even for me. But at night...

"Go ahead and say it," I snap, and he glances up from where he's saddling Racia.

I'm doing the same to Kazi, and she turns her head, narrowing one eye at my tone.

"Oh, give it a rest," I tell her. "You'd be pissed, too, if you had to deal with him all day."

Rakiz raises one eyebrow, looking rumpled but relaxed. I feel the opposite and could use another few hours of sleep.

"Say what?" he asks mildly, turning back to the mishua.

"Don't play with me."

"Fine. Why do you cry in your sleep?"

I flinch, and the mishua throws her head. Rakiz jolts forward, but I've already jumped out of the way. Just like that, Rakiz is no longer the laid-back version of himself. He pulls me close, and I can feel his chest rumbling as he growls at the mishua.

She immediately bows her head, contrite, and I feel my eyebrows almost hit my hairline at the quick change. This is the side of Rakiz that everyone always sees. The tribe king.

He lets me go, and I turn.

"You can saddle the damn mishua," I say, and surprisingly he does it. The mishua is as sweet as a baby calf, nuzzling him as if looking for his affection. He ignores her, obviously still pissed.

"Are you planning to answer the question?"

I clear my throat. Hiding it just makes it a bigger deal. "Our platoon was attacked in Baghdad—a city in a country called Iraq. We received bad intel about the strength and size of the enemy forces."

Rakiz finishes with the mishua and gives her one stroke on the nose before turning back to me. The words are harder to get out when those dark eyes are staring into mine, so I turn away, packing up our camp.

"We were ambushed. Three of my friends died instantly. I watched a fourth bleed out while I lay trapped underneath the Humvee. My leg was pinned, so I was just waiting to die."

I can feel Rakiz move closer, and I'm not at all surprised when he wraps his arms around me. Strangely this gives me the strength I need to keep going.

"I was taken as a prisoner of war with my best friend."

Rakiz is silent behind me, but his arms tighten slightly, giving me the strength I need to continue.

"Jack was my rock. I'd lost my brother to a drug overdose a few years earlier, although I hadn't seen him since he'd split when he was seventeen. Jack kind of filled that empty spot. He was hilarious, the kind of person who just brings everyone together, you know?"

Rakiz nods, bending until his chin rests on my head. I'm surrounded by his huge body, keeping me safe from the memories.

I shake off that thought. No. Relying on anyone else is a bad idea.

My tone is business-like when I continue, but I have to wipe my sweaty palms on my pants. I tell myself Rakiz hasn't noticed, but he will have. He notices everything.

"We were locked up together. I would've given them anything they wanted if they had just left him alone." I finish that last sentence in a whisper, shame hitting me in the gut. Jack was my family, and I failed him.

"If he is the man you describe him as, he would never have blamed you. You understand this, right?" Rakiz's voice is low, sympathy coating his words.

I nod. Jack's last words to me?

"Don't tell them anything, Vada. Don't you dare say a fucking word."

They must have known we had nothing to tell them. We were lower enlisted. So they sent the usual video back to the states, threatening to cut off our heads. And when the US government didn't move fast enough...

"They killed him," I choke out. "And then they left me there to rot."

I shrug out of Rakiz's hold and stride toward the mishua. I can feel his gaze on me as I haul myself onto her back, but I stare into the trees until he finally mounts Racia.

We're silent for the next few hours, but I'm not stupid enough to think Rakiz will leave the subject alone. The guy is like a dog with a bone.

We reach the edge of the forest, and I stare into the distance.

"At least there's only one way to go from here," I say.

We couldn't be more vulnerable, and I can practically hear Rakiz grinding his teeth next to me as look at the route in front of us.

There are no more trees, no shelter—nothing to hide us from Voildi, enemy warriors, or other predators.

I sigh. "Let's stretch our legs and have something to eat."

I'm dying to pee, and I duck around a tree while Rakiz secures the mishua, reaching for rations.

"Where do you think they're taking them?" I ask when I return, rinsing my hands with some of the water we refilled.

He gives me a look. "Where do *you* think they're taking them?"

I raise an eyebrow but pull out my map. He stares at it over my shoulder, and I glance back at his face. He looks torn between laughing and roaring with rage at the sight of it.

"I did my homework," I tell him.

"I don't know what homework is, but you prepared well. How did you get this? My warriors know better than to allow you to mine them for information."

I sniff, refusing to throw Ellie and Vivian under the bus. "I have my ways."

I examine the map, which has smeared terribly even though I've been careful with it. By now, I almost know it by heart though, and I frown down at it. "We're leaving the

Seinex Forest now, right? My guess is that the Voildi took them to Nexia. Is the slave market still dismantled?"

Rakiz is silent, and I glance back to see him staring at me.

"You are a dangerous female," he says, and I grin.

"Glad you finally recognize. So...is it?"

"I sent Tagiz and Hewex to check—which I see you already know." He sounds disgusted, and I feel my grin widen. "They hadn't returned when I left," he says.

"Even if it's dismantled, the Voildi could sell the women privately, right?"

Rakiz nods. "I wouldn't have thought a pack of Voildi would have the intelligence to do so, but if they were able to stalk the other pack, steal the women, conceal their movements from my warriors...females are worth much on this planet."

I nod. "Good. If they've been sold, they're still alive."

I put away my map, shaking out my legs. I'm not used to riding for days at a time, and my whole body aches.

"Would you have returned to my camp once you found these women?"

I turn warily, heeding the danger in Rakiz's voice. "Eventually," I say honestly. "After we rescued Charlie and Alexis."

His jaw tightens. "And then what?"

"And then we'd have left." My voice is even, and I throw up my hands. "Is this seriously news to you?"

He narrows his eyes, the relaxed man long gone. I'm staring at the tribe king again, and for some reason, which I can't quite put my finger on, it pisses me off.

"When I tumble you, you will change your mind."

I laugh. "Let me get this straight. You think I'll give up the one opportunity I have to get back to *my world* for sex?"

He just stares at me, and then his gaze moves over my

body insolently. I raise an eyebrow, unwilling to let him see exactly what that gaze does to me.

"Oh, sweetie," I say with a wince. "You may be good, but no one's *that* good."

To my surprise, he smiles, the look in his eyes promising all kinds of dirty things. The kinds of dirty things that my pussy is hoping he can back up. It's been a long time.

I glance away. There are more than enough men available to scratch my itch on Earth. Sex with Rakiz would be an incredibly dumb move.

He shifts, drawing my eyes back to him, and I sigh.

"You don't want me because you desire me as a woman, Rakiz. You want me because you see me as a challenge. Because I'm the only woman you know who isn't throwing herself at you."

He grits his teeth. "You're sure about that, are you?"

"Yeah. So let me be clear. Find that challenge elsewhere. I don't have time for you."

He steps forward, eyes darkening, and a shiver runs down my spine.

"Let *me* be clear. I want you, and I'll have you. I'm a very patient male. I have time to wait out your hand-wringing."

Hand-wringing?

This male was put on this planet to drive me insane.

I narrow my eyes but turn away. I know better than to engage with crazy. I ignore his low laugh and get back on my mishua, pushing the thought of sex with him out of my head.

Sometimes a woman looks at a man, and she's pretty sure the sex would be good. Something in the way he walks, talks, moves, or even just looks at her tells her that he'd probably know his way around her body.

With Rakiz, I *know* the sex would be better than good. In

fact, there's not a doubt in my mind that the sex would be excellent.

The problem? I wouldn't just be sleeping with Rakiz. I'd also be sleeping with the tribe king.

I wait for Rakiz to mount, still annoyed that my moody mishua is tied to his. Then we head out into the open.

CHAPTER EIGHT

Nevada

We ride hard. If I thought the mishua was a bumpy ride before we picked up the pace, I had no idea what I was in for. At one point, Rakiz glances over his shoulder, taking in my clenched teeth and white knuckles as I hold on for dear life. He opens his mouth, likely to tell me to get onto his mishua with him, and I glower at him. He snaps his mouth shut, sends me a wicked grin, and picks up the pace.

Wise guy.

We're sitting ducks out here, and the mishua are behaving like assholes, likely picking up on our tension.

Kazi sidesteps, and I curse. Rakiz growls a warning, and the mishua falls back in line.

"Could you kiss his ass any harder?" I mutter to her, and she bristles, practically vibrating with the need to throw me off. Rakiz narrows his eyes.

"Behave," he says.

I don't know if he's talking to me or the mishua, and I stick my tongue out at him. His eyes darken, his lips curling up at the corners.

"Be careful. I might take that as an invitation."

Rakiz glances around, and we pick up the speed again. Neither of us want to be out here when the sun goes down. Apparently there's a small cave used by the warriors when they're on hunting trips. If we can get to it tonight, we can get up early and move into Nexia before the sun is high in the sky.

That's the plan anyway.

There are a few trees in the distance when Rakiz slows his mishua to a walk. My mishua follows suit, and I'm opening my mouth to ask what's going on when I feel it.

"Someone's watching us," I say, and he nods.

"We did well to get this far. Let's feign obliviousness. You are so enamored with your warrior that you have eyes only for him, and I am so determined to have you in my furs that I have no idea of the threat to our safety."

I laugh, letting the sound carry as if I don't have a care in the world. I carefully ignore the tiny burst of heat in my chest at the idea of Rakiz being *my* warrior.

He grins at me, but I'd have to be an idiot to think that his grin is real.

His eyes are hard as stone, vowing retribution to anyone that comes close, and I watch as he lowers his gaze, probably aware that he looks like a serial killer.

I blow out a breath and then make a stupid comment about the weather. I'm wearing my cloak, and whoever is watching us will discount me, not expecting me to be armed.

We also have the mishua, who can apparently be vicious in battle.

"Do you think they know who you are?" I murmur to Rakiz and then throw my head back, laughing as if he's told a particularly funny joke.

He shrugs. "It's hard to know. I was a well-known warrior at one time." A cloud comes over his face, and then it clears. "But I haven't hunted for years."

He grins at me again, and I roll my eyes.

"Your acting could sure use some work, buddy."

We stick to a walk for a while and then pick up the pace slightly. For whatever reason, whoever is watching us is choosing not to attack now. Instead, they're lying in wait—likely preparing a trap.

I grind my teeth. This planet gives a whole new meaning to the word *inhospitable*. Sure, there's food, water, and oxygen, but the locals have a major obsession with killing each other.

They wait until we're almost at the tree line, not far from where Rakiz told me we'll be sleeping tonight. A cold sweat forms on the back of my neck when they surround us.

This pack of Voildi is larger than the one that pretended to rescue us. It took three warriors to fight them off, and we just have the two of us.

Shit.

Voildi have skin the color of urine and sharp, pointed teeth designed for tearing meat from the bone.

One of them steps forward. He's larger than the others, and his hair is cut close to his scalp, revealing a long scar that twists along the side of his head.

I glance at Rakiz, and he looks cool and unconcerned. He raises his eyebrow as he stares down his nose at the leader.

"You made a mistake coming here," Scar says. "This is our territory."

I can picture Jack, up in heaven or wherever he is, laughing at this guy's bad lines.

Rakiz snorts. "You have no territory. You are a pest just waiting to be eradicated."

This pisses them off. There must be twelve Voildi here, and they step forward, murder in their eyes.

One of them gets too close to Racia, and she lashes out. Rakiz sits on her back with a placid expression as she rears, striking with her feet, and I gape as she runs the Voildi down, then gouges him with her horns until he's lying twitching on the ground, choking on blood.

Wow.

The other Voildi attack as one. I stay on the mishua for now, although that may not be for long, since she pays no attention to my attempts to steer her and instead charges at one of the Voildi like a bull.

A Voildi head goes flying, and Rakiz roars in triumph, a savage grin on his face. I take a moment to stare. He looks more alive in this moment than any time I've seen him so far.

The Voildi manages to dodge my mishua, so I run him through with my sword.

The mishua chooses not to wait around for me to pull my sword out and instead keeps moving.

"You bitch," I growl as I jump off. It's either that or lose my sword. I pull it free and turn, immediately dodging a horizontal stab. I punch the attacker in the face and slide my sword into his gut.

Then Rakiz is there, beheading him for me. I scowl at the easy movement. I'm only so strong, and my sword is only so big. With Rakiz's huge arms and heavy, flat sword, he can smoothly decapitate the Voildi as they approach.

We turn as one, fighting back to back. Rakiz has been

busy while I was occupied, and there are only eight of them left.

The next few seconds stretch into minutes as we're attacked from both sides. I thank whatever god is listening that Asroz gave up so much of his time to train me, but I'm barely dodging their blows. One of them lunges forward, striking at my stomach, and I step back, turning. I swipe my blade along his arm, and his sword falls to the ground.

Along with his hand.

He screams, and I whirl away, parrying another strike. The force vibrates up my arm, and I grit my teeth as I kick out at knee level. These aliens may look different, but most of their parts seem to be where mine are, and I grin as his knee buckles and he stumbles into my fist.

"Nevada!" Rakiz's roar is guttural, and I jolt back, barely saving my head. He's fighting his way back toward me, and I can't pinpoint the moment we got separated. He's not having fun anymore. His eyes are full of fury and terror. For me.

We may actually die here.

I grit my teeth, striking out at the Voildi as he gets too close. I'm slowing down though, and he easily bats my sword away, grinning through sharp teeth.

"You dare fight with a sword, female? We will put your head on a pike as a warning to any who would think to do the same."

"Yeah, yeah. Bring it."

He looks confused for a moment but then scowls, moving faster than I anticipated. He grins, his gaze flicking over my shoulder, and I duck as Rakiz's hard body slams into me.

I hit the ground hard, attempting to roll to my feet, but there's nowhere to go. Rakiz is on his knees, sheltering me, teeth bared, sword in his hand.

"Give us the female, and we will let you fight another day."

Rakiz laughs, and the Voildi attack.

This is it. I get to my knees as well, hand wrapped tightly around my sword.

Rakiz parries the first strike, and the Voildi stumbles, coming close enough for me to slice my sword along the backs of his knees. He crumples, and Rakiz takes his head.

"Rakiz!" I scream, lunging forward, but I'm too far, and the Voildi is too fast.

A high-pitched shriek sounds, and the Voildi turns as Racia gores him with her horns, picking him up and shaking her head. He dies instantly, one of her horns through his chest.

"No," Rakiz snarls, but it's too late. Racia can't see past the body hanging from her head, and one of the Voildi lunges forward, slicing her open. His sword gets stuck in her scales, but he managed to hit her vulnerable underbelly, and she goes down.

The remaining Voildi laugh, and I choke out a sob even as I lift my sword. Even with Rakiz fighting like he's possessed, we're hopelessly outnumbered. Of all the ways I've imagined dying, this never made the list.

The air fills with the sound of roaring, and I glance at Rakiz, but he's silent, his sword in his hand as he jumps from his knees to his feet.

Within seconds, the remaining Voildi are dispatched, and I stare, mouth open as their heads hit the ground.

We're surrounded by mishua, and I manage to make it to my feet, teeth bared.

"Stand down, Nevada." Rakiz's voice is tired. "They're my men."

Rakiz

I kneel next to Racia as the light slowly goes out of her eyes. "Thank you, old friend."

She snuffles my hand as I pat her snout and closes her eyes for the last time. Beside me, Nevada chokes back a sob.

"I'm sorry," she says, and I turn, wrapping my arm around her. I scan her body, relief running through me. She's bruised, but none of her injuries seem to be anything that won't heal within a few days.

"Sorry for what?"

She runs her hand over one of the mishua's horns. "If I hadn't stolen her, she wouldn't have died."

I place my hand over hers. "She died the way a mishua would want to—in battle. I was the one who was slowly killing her, leaving her to wither in her pen."

I feel Nevada's eyes on me, and I swallow around a lump in my throat. Warriors do not cry. And yet I will mourn Racia, who fought with me through so many battles before I became king.

Part of me wonders if she chose this death. If she knew that once we returned to camp, she would once again be back in her pen. Guilt stabs through me, and Nevada leans her head against my chest, a silent show of support.

We're surrounded by death, and I need to take Nevada away from this place. I get to my feet, pulling her with me, and nod at my warriors, who have waited silently while I say my goodbyes.

"Tagiz and Hewex, this is Nevada."

They nod at each other, and I turn to find my other mishua snuffling at her fallen friend. She is covered in blood, and I lean forward, examining her head, but none of the blood seems to be hers.

"You look like you enjoyed yourself," I murmur, and she snorts, moving close so I can give her a stroke.

"You're bleeding," Nevada says, her hands quick as she pushes my torn shirt aside.

"It's nothing to be concerned about," I say. The wound is shallow, and while it burns, the bleeding will stop soon.

I turn back to Hewex. "How did you find us?"

The warrior is old and grizzled. He never found a mate and so spends all his time away from camp. He once told me his love of females could never match his love of a good fight.

Not long ago, I believed the same. I glance at Nevada, who is examining both of the warriors with cool eyes. I smile and then glance back at Hewex, who stands straighter at my regard.

"We were on our way back to camp after our travels to Nexia," he says. "We heard sounds of a battle."

"Like catnip, right?" Nevada mutters, and we all glance at her. "Never mind."

"What did you find in Nexia?"

Tagiz frowns. "The slave market is still dismantled, but according to the rumors, it has merely been driven underground."

As expected. I grit my teeth. "I know you have probably been hoping to get back to camp and rest, but I need you to come back to Nexia with us."

"Of course." They both nod.

I stare down at Racia for one last moment. I would like to bury her, but we have no tools with us, and we need to get to shelter as soon as possible. It's likely that these Voildi are part of a larger pack, who will send out a search party when they don't return.

Nevada slides her hand into mine as I stroke Racia's snout one last time.

"My father allowed me to choose from a litter of mishua when I was a child. Racia was the only one who didn't immediately beg for my attention. She seemed unimpressed by me."

Nevada laughs and wipes away a tear. "Yeah, I can imagine she made you work for her respect."

"She died a warrior's death," Hewex says softly, and I nod.

I turn and lift Nevada onto the other mishua, who is solemn and placid. I mount behind her, and we leave the death behind us.

Nevada is quiet as we make our way to the cave, and Tagiz and Hewex fill me in on what they found in Nexia. The area has long been a cesspool. It was first a trading post for goods before it drew the attention of too many criminals. Eventually the Voildi took a corner of the territory for themselves, and numerous other creatures joined the fray, bargaining for things that they had no business bargaining for.

No matter what you want on this planet, you can find it in Nexia. Dexar may have shut down one slave market, but I have no doubt that there are still many more operating underground.

The center of Nexia is called Sebe, and it's the closest to anything passing for neutral territory in this region of Agron. I feel my lips curl as I glance at Nevada. She will enjoy the market. I can picture her glancing around with curious eyes.

She's still pale, and I don't miss the concern in her gaze

as she glances back at the cut on my arm. My shoulders straighten. The hardheaded female cares. She cares more than she would like to admit.

I suppress a satisfied grin, tuning back into Hewex and Tagiz's conversation. Their voices are a low murmur, and we walk through the edge of the forest quietly. This is a small forest bordering Nexia, where it would be suicide to go after dark without more warriors, especially while bleeding. I feel my shoulders relax when we finally reach the cave.

"We stayed here on the way to Nexia," Tagiz says. "And we refilled the supplies after our visit to the market."

I nod in approval. We have many similar shelters scattered across our territory and even a few hidden deep within the Voildi territories. Some we even share with other Braxian tribes. The rules are simple. Leave more than you found in the shelter.

If there were four furs, bring an extra one back. Always ensure there are enough supplies for a warrior who could be hurt, and never eat more than you need.

We tether the mishua at the entrance to the cave. We stopped for water on the way here, and there are several large buckets already filled in the cave.

Nevada looks at one longingly, and I feel the corner of my mouth turn up. I nod to the back corner of the cave. "I will hold up a pelt to provide cover if you'd like to bathe."

She tilts her head, and Tagiz shifts. "We will go back to the river to bathe. You can use the water. Hewex and I will take turns on sentry duty."

"I can do a shift," Nevada offers, and Tagiz glances at me.

"They're familiar with this area," I say. "They'll immediately know if a particular sound is an animal commonly found here or someone sneaking up on us. You should rest."

Nevada opens her mouth but surprisingly, she shrugs.

From the circles beneath her eyes, I'm guessing she realizes just how badly she needs to sleep.

We share rations and build a fire, which quickly warms the cave. Then Tagiz and Hewex nod at us and depart for the night. They will likely make their own camp close by but in an area better suited to see and hear anyone attempting to sneak up on us.

I pull the buckets away from our sleeping area and move them close to the back of the cave, where the water will run away from the entrance. Then I pull off my shirt while Nevada sharpens her sword, no doubt carefully ignoring me while I wash.

"Are you ready?" I ask, and she nods, placing her sword down and reaching for the small ball of soap. I hold the thick pelt above my head, mulling over the fact that I'm once again listening to the sound of Nevada's splashes and sighs.

When she's finished, she dries herself with a fur and then pulls on the shirt she sleeps in. My shirt. The one she took with her even when she thought she might never see me again.

I grit my teeth and try to ignore the outline of her nipples, hard beneath the material. She stares up at me for a long moment, and we're both silent.

The words come out before I'm even aware of them.

"One night." My voice is hoarse. "And if you wish, we will never speak of it again."

Nevada

I stare at Rakiz. His hands are clenched into fists as if he's barely holding himself back from touching me. His face is hard, and he's looking at me like I'm the answer to every question he's ever had.

We both almost died today. Suddenly the thought of one or both of us no longer breathing without acting on the incredible chemistry that sparks between us...it's incomprehensible.

No regrets. If I leave and I don't know how it feels when Rakiz is inside me, I'll think about it for the rest of my life.

"Fine," I say. "One night. But that's it."

He nods slowly, and then he whips out his hand, burying it in my hair as he pulls me close, kissing me deeply. He steals my breath, and I gasp against him as he lifts me up and strides back into his sleeping area.

His hands are everywhere, sliding over my body, under my shirt, his skin warm against mine.

I want more. So much more.

"You'll want me for more than one night, my stubborn female. And if you're very good, I'll let you have me."

I laugh as he places me down on his furs. "You arrogant ass."

He grins down at me, and my breath hitches. I feel so fortunate to see this side of him. The relaxed, playful side that no one else gets to see.

It feels like a gift.

Rakiz nibbles at my lower lip gently, asking permission this time. He's like a lion pretending to be a kitten, and I'm not fooled. But I open anyway, and he strokes my tongue with his, a low growl escaping.

I shiver at the sound, desperate for him to make it again. I want to make this man lose his mind.

I'm suddenly impatient, ready for him to be inside me. I grasp at him, pulling him close as I wrestle with his shirt. He lets out a choked laugh, ripping it off, and then he moves back, staring down at me intently.

"I like you in my shirt," he says, and then he reaches down and rips it from my body.

I scowl at him. "That was my nightgown."

"I'll give you a new one," he promises, leaning down to nuzzle my breasts.

I inhale sharply as he takes my nipple into his mouth, shuddering as I bury my hands in his hair. Rakiz leans up, catching my arms and trapping them above my head, my wrists prisoners in one of his huge hands.

His other hand slides down, pushing my thighs apart, and then he bends his head, stroking me with his tongue.

"God..."

He licks and sucks, and everything fades away except for the pressure building in my pussy. I unravel, crying out as I writhe, and Rakiz continues licking, drawing out my pleasure until I'm a puddle beneath him.

"Look at me, Nevada."

I crack open my eyes and blink up at him, and then I'm gasping as he slides inside me, filling me up the way I've been fantasizing about since the moment I met him.

He's hot and hard, rolling his hips as he thrusts against me. I shudder as he moves one hand underneath my butt, angling me so he can get deeper, hitting the spot that makes me moan. I clutch at his back, the huge muscles bulging as he moves within me, and the thought of his giant, magnificent body bringing me so much pleasure tips me over.

I tremble, opening my mouth on a choked cry as my orgasm hits, and Rakiz continues rocking against me as another orgasm makes me moan, my nails raking down his back.

Rakiz thrusts deep, an almost pained groan leaving him

as he empties within me.

"Wow," I gasp when I can speak again. "There's sex, and then there's *sex*. Go team."

He lets out a choked laugh and then rolls, pulling me close until I'm sprawling over his chest.

We relax in contented silence for a few minutes, and I almost fall asleep as Rakiz trails his fingers up and down my back. I feel lethargic and energized, exhausted and invigorated all at once. Tomorrow I'll examine the repercussions of what we've just done. But tonight I'm just going to enjoy the fact that some of the tension that I carry each day has straight up disappeared.

"Do you like being king?" I ask suddenly, then immediately clamp my mouth shut. I'm not sure why I felt the need to ask, and I shift, ready to move away.

Rakiz's arm clamps down like a vice, holding me to him. It's gentle until I attempt to wiggle away.

I lift my head and glower at him. He smiles at me, wagging his eyebrows, and he looks like a mischievous little boy. "If you stay exactly where you are, perhaps I'll tell you."

I roll my eyes. "I'm comfortable anyway," I say, laying my head back on his chest.

He laughs, that big chest shaking. "You could be stuck in the desert for two days and still not admit that you're thirsty, karja."

I shrug. "I am who I am."

"And I like who you are."

"What does *karja* mean?"

"A karja is a fierce animal—one that no warrior wants to find when alone in the wild. But very rarely—if shown enough affection—they will deign to eat from a warrior's hand. It takes many years, but once tamed, a karja will be forever loyal to their warrior."

I can hear the smile in his voice, and it makes me bite my lip. When did we go from hating each other to snuggling after sex? How did Rakiz move from wanting to strangle me to liking who I am?

"What's wrong?"

I voice my thoughts, and he laughs again. "Oh, I'm sure I'll want to strangle you again soon."

I reach up and roughly pinch his nipple, and he mutters a curse as he reaches down and pinches my ass cheek.

"Hey!"

"I never wanted to be king," he says, his hand stroking over my butt.

"Really?"

I feel him nod. "I was never someone who wanted to rule. I would have been more than content with a life as a warrior or even a trader. I think I might even have enjoyed working with the mishua more. Especially if a certain human female was being punished with the same task."

His voice is low and teasing, and I can't help but grin against him.

"So why do you do it? Why not let someone else rule?"

"I thought about it. When my father died, I was immediately called back from camp. My father had recognized that if he didn't allow me to live as a warrior while I was younger, something inside me would die. And he was wise enough to understand that a king who rules warriors needs to know exactly what it means to live as a warrior. So I was given more freedom than anyone approved of, and I appreciated each and every moment away from camp. When I was hunting or fighting, I wasn't next in line for the throne. I was just another warrior, proving myself like every other male."

"But then he died."

Rakiz heaves a sigh. "Yes."

"Unexpectedly."

"Yes. It was so minor. He was bitten by a haliea—a poisonous creature. They're not hunters but are extremely territorial—especially if their nests are threatened."

Rakiz's whole body is tense, and I raise my head. He's staring at the roof of the cave as if he wants to commit murder.

"He could've lived. If the stubborn bastard had just gone to the healer's tent. But he decided he knew better. No one knew what had happened until he was too late. He died in excruciating pain, without any family close."

I swallow around the lump in my throat. Rakiz's voice is stark with pain.

"Where was your mom?"

"Dead."

Nice going, Nevada. Make the guy even more depressed.

"I'm so sorry, Rakiz."

He nods, and I crawl up his body until I can press a kiss against his jaw. He seems to come back from whatever dark place he was visiting because he slides his hand into my hair, holding my head still while he takes my mouth possessively.

"How old were you?" I ask when he allows me to pull away.

"I had seen sixteen summers."

Jesus. Sixteen years old, and he was suddenly responsible for a tribe of close to a thousand people, all of whom were in mourning.

He rolls me beneath him suddenly, and I blink up at him.

"Enough talking of the past." He leans down and takes my mouth, hands wandering over my body, and I groan. He may be right. One night may not be enough.

CHAPTER NINE

N*evada*

THE MARKET IS LIKE NOTHING I'VE EVER SEEN BEFORE. I'VE been to many markets in the Middle East and United States —even one in Thailand when Jake insisted we make the most of our leave.

But none of them compare to this.

The kradis rise high on each side of a thoroughfare and are likely used for storing goods and protecting the vendors from the midday sun. Merchant stalls sit in rows, offering perfume, paints, jewelry, food, clothing, ornate furniture, and even small creatures in cages.

There are many different aliens here. I see no Braxians, but some of the creatures are feathered or furry and wearing armor, cloth, or nothing at all. The breeze brings a complex aroma to me—one of cooked food and heady spices along with the nose-wrinkling scent of hundreds of people in a small space.

We walk through the market, the warriors stopping every so often to ask questions about potential sightings of the other human women.

Here, Rakiz isn't a king. With his face a mess of bruises and his outfit one that's seen better days, he's just a man. A man who keeps me close, holding me protectively—not because he doesn't think I can look after myself but because he sees it as his privilege.

This side of Rakiz is impossible to ignore. He's quick to smile, laughing with his men even as his eyes continually scan our surroundings. He flashes me the occasional grin, stopping to talk to sellers and complimenting them on their wares.

"What do you need today?" a vendor asks, and I almost snort. No one *needs* the glimmering ropes of gold, the jeweled rings, or the bracelets with their precious stones. But there's no question that her wares are beautiful.

Rakiz has his eyes on a particularly gorgeous bracelet. I want to elbow him and tell him that if he truly wants it, he needs to be less obvious about it. Right now the stall owner is practically rubbing her hands together in glee as his dark gaze caresses the piece.

It gleams gold, with tiny stones that remind me of Australian opals of differing sizes. The stones are placed at irregular intervals, ensuring that once your gaze hits the bracelet, you don't want to look away.

The ends of the bracelet are curved in a swirled pattern, and I frown, unsure how it would be worn. While the top swirl would sit along the forearm, the bottom one would need to lie against the top of the hand.

"How much?" Rakiz asks. Then he lets loose the grin that never appeared at camp. The one that invites the receiver of that grin to play with him.

The seller's eyes light up, and the bargaining begins.

A few minutes later, I'm struggling to not roll my eyes. The seller and Rakiz have gone to war. A war with words that vary from thinly veiled insults to backhanded compliments.

"I had not realized this market had descended to daylight robbery," Rakiz says at one point.

"I had not realized you were hurting for credits, araz," the woman replies with a smirk, and Rakiz's eyes narrow as mine widen. I've heard this word before.

Araz is a slang word for *king*. Somehow, this woman knows exactly who Rakiz is. If that annoys Rakiz or makes him nervous in any way, no one would know it. A slow smile crawls across his face, and he nods to her as if accepting her point.

Rakiz says something that my translator doesn't pick up, and the woman throws her head back with a laugh. She glances at me, eyes twinkling, and I raise an eyebrow.

She murmurs something back to Rakiz, and I use the time to check out some of the stalls surrounding us.

There. Those pieces of fabric look surprisingly familiar. I narrow my eyes, then turn as Rakiz takes my elbow, steering me into a corner that's a little quieter.

"What's up?" I smile as I note the bracelet in his hand. "Aw, did you get your bling, your majesty?"

He gives me a look that suggests I may just be the dumbest person on this planet. "I got *your* bling, karja."

I grin at the sound of Rakiz saying the word *bling*. There's no translation for the word, so he mangles the English until it's almost unrecognizable.

Then I frown. "Wait, what?"

He gives me an impatient look, and his hand tightens

slightly on my elbow as if he's worried I'll suddenly yank my arm away.

Today I'm wearing the one piece of clothing I managed to salvage after the crash—my blank tank top. I've covered it with one of the warrior's vests, which the seamstress somehow cut down and tailored to fit me, leaving my arms bare.

"I can't—"

Rakiz ignores me, keeping my arm in his. I raise a brow as he gently maneuvers the bracelet, opening it slightly until he can slide it over my wrist, then up and over my elbow.

Once it circles my bicep, he presses it closed, and I blink down at it.

Oh. It's not a bracelet at all.

It's completely stunning. The gold gleams against my skin, exquisite in its simplicity. The stones catch the light, but instead of screaming "look at me," they complement the gold.

I don't wear a lot of jewelry. But it's like Rakiz reached into my brain and then chose the exact piece I would fall in love with.

"I can't take this, Rakiz—"

He simply smiles at me, and his fingers stroke over the cool metal and caress my upper arm.

"This was made for you, my warrior female." His gaze scans my body and then returns to my face, satisfaction in his eyes at whatever he sees there.

He leans close, gaze falling to my lips as he bends down. He doesn't kiss me though. Instead, he waits patiently for me. I scowl at him even as I reach out, grab his shirt, and pull him to me, shoving every ounce of my confused frustration into our kiss.

Someone clears their throat, and Rakiz slowly moves his

head back. The corner of his mouth lifts as he studies me intently, and to my shock, I'm almost blushing.

What the hell is happening to me? I move away, and Rakiz allows the retreat even as his eyes follow me. Tagiz clears his throat again, amusement clear on his face as I give him a look.

"We have asked all our contacts, and no one is talking," he says.

Rakiz frowns, once again all business. "Do you think they're scared or that they truly don't know?"

Tagiz shrugs. "I'm not sure. Anyone who trades in this area is both well aware of the brutality of the Voildi and likely to avoid making enemies."

I frown, frustrated. While the guys talk, I wander over to the vendor with the strange pieces of material. I can feel Rakiz's eyes on me as he talks strategy, and I ignore the way my heart flips. He may be an overprotective barbarian, but something about having his focus on me makes my thighs clench and my stomach flutter.

"See something you like?"

The vendor is a male with light-blue skin and slitted eyes. His head is completely bald; in fact, it seems as if he has no hair anywhere on his body. His skin is almost pore-less, making him appear a little like a wax doll.

"What are these?" I narrow my eyes as I examine the shimmery blue-green material—the same blue-green as the scales along Rakiz's chest and shoulders. Each one is about twice the size of a laptop, and I raise an eyebrow as I look back up at the vendor, who grins at me, showcasing a disturbing number of teeth.

How do so many teeth even fit inside his mouth?

I shake off that thought and reach out, stroking a finger down the material.

Oh, wow.

"These are scales," I say, and the vendor nods.

"What from?"

He gives me the same look that Rakiz just gave me, and I scowl at him. I'm getting real tired of men silently implying that I'm a particularly dense kind of stupid.

"They're dragon scales, aren't they?"

He nods.

"How many dragons are there?"

He tilts his head, and my scowl deepens.

"I'm not from around here, okay? So enough with the attitude."

He examines me for a long moment and then finally laughs. "There is just one. Dragix, our—"

"Great ancestor," I finish. "Got it. Where did you find them?"

He laughs again. "If I were to tell people where to find these beauties, I would have no business. They would simply find them and keep them or sell them themselves."

A woman appears, standing behind the stall. She looks exactly like the guy I'm talking to, only she's wearing a small cloth that barely covers three large breasts.

"I don't want to do either of those things," I say. "Our friend is missing. We believe she was taken by Dragix. If we can narrow down the dragon's recent movements, we might be able to find her."

Both of them study me for a long moment. Then the man's eyes drop to my bicep.

"I may be willing to trade," he says softly.

I slap my hand over my new bracelet—arm cuff. Whatever.

"You can't have this," I snap, and his eyes narrow in offense. I blow out a breath and gesture to where Rakiz is still in conversation with Tagiz and Hewex. He meets my eyes even as he responds to whatever Hewex is saying.

"See that guy?" I gesture toward the group, and the man nods. "He'd be willing to trade with you."

The man sizes up Rakiz, and I almost vibrate with impatience. Rakiz glances past me, meeting the man's eyes and raising his eyebrow.

I almost laugh. Rakiz is dressed in battle leathers with three days of beard growth and tousled hair. But his head is held high, his gaze hard, and the imperious look on his face leaves no doubt that he's a ruler.

The woman sucks in a breath.

"Araz," she murmurs, and I meet her eyes. We're incognito here for a reason. It's not a good idea for people in this area to find out that not only is the king away from his tribe, but he only has two warriors with him.

I turn back to Rakiz and gesture him over. The woman sucks in another breath, and her eyes widen as Rakiz strides to us.

"So," I say as he arrives, "these guys know where Dragix has been recently. Unfortunately, this man is unwilling to give us the information freely," I say, and Rakiz bares his teeth at the man in a feral smile.

The woman flinches, and if she were human, I'd half expect her to make the sign of the cross as she stares at Rakiz.

The man is less impressed. His face goes a lighter shade of blue, but he firms his jaw. "I am sure you appreciate the importance of confidentiality for my business."

Rakiz nods. "And how much to buy a piece of that confidentiality?"

The man's jaw bulges as he grits his teeth. "Twenty-five credits."

I have no idea how much that is on this planet or what it could buy. But the woman's mouth drops open when Rakiz simply nods, reaches into his pocket, and hands over the money.

The man stares at us for a long moment, and I sigh.

"The woman who went missing...she looks like me. We aren't from this planet. We were stranded here and separated. I need to find her. Please."

The man blinks his slitted eyes and then nods. He turns his head, scanning our surroundings as he lowers his voice. Rakiz gestures to Tagiz and Hewex, who move close to the vendors' stand, crossing their arms and staring down anyone who thinks to come close.

I sigh. *Subtle, guys. Real subtle.*

The man switches to another language, and I scowl as I realize my translator is only picking up every third or fourth word.

I rub my ear, but the language is either too old or a dialect that the translator hasn't been programmed for.

Rakiz nods, and they talk for a few more minutes. I take out my crude map and hand it to Rakiz, but he waves it off and taps one finger against his head, finishing up his conversation with the man.

The woman eyes my map.

"You are searching for more than one female?"

I nod. "Have you...seen anyone else who looks like me?"

Her eyes widen slightly as she also scans the immediate area for eavesdroppers. I sigh. If anyone happens to be watching us from afar, there will be no doubt in their mind that we're talking about something we don't want overheard.

"My sister was traveling on the outskirts of Sebe. She has two children who need medicine that can only be found in the prexas." She smiles slightly at my confusion. "Passageways built underground. Centuries ago, Agron was engulfed by a war. For years, to travel above ground was suicide as different factions and races fought to take control of the largest territory possible. And so prexas were originally built as a way for everyday citizens to safely get from place to place."

"What are they used for now?"

Her mouth twists. "They are used by both the desperate and the evil. My sister's children could be cured with a large enough dose of yurian—the medicine she must buy each week. However, she does not have enough money to buy the doses in full. Whenever she gets close, the sellers seem to universally raise the prices that week. She cannot risk attempting to cure one child because if the other was to go even a week without the medicine they need...the death is said to be excruciating," she whispers.

"Those motherfuckers." Nothing pisses me off more than those who prey on the weak. There's a special place in hell for people who would keep a woman from saving her children's lives simply so she'll have to continue paying them each week.

She nods. "These are the types of people found in the prexas. Those who would kill each other if they came upon one another alone and defenseless yet would collaborate to keep people like my sister in incredible poverty."

Rakiz is silent beside me, letting me take the lead, and I appreciate it.

"So your sister saw someone who looked like me?"

She nods again. "She had two legs, two arms, and pale skin. My sister noticed because she wore thin clothes and had dull teeth and no claws."

My heart races as my stomach swims at the thought of one of the women being so defenseless in a place like that.

"The woman was alone?"

"Yes." She frowns, staring into space for a moment before she clicks her fingers with a grin that displays rows of pointed teeth. Her claws slide off each other, making a slight screeching sound. "Hair like fire," she blurts. "That's why my sister thought to mention the female to me. She said her hair looked like fire."

I turn to Rakiz. "Ivy has red hair."

He nods, but his eyes are still on the woman. "How much is the medicine to cure both children?"

The woman's grin fades. "One hundred credits," she murmurs softly. "Each."

I scowl. "How much do they charge her each week?"

"Ten credits for each child. That is usually enough for them to get through the week, although sometimes they fall ill right before their next dose."

Twenty credits a week. And this guy seemed stunned that Rakiz paid twenty-five for information. No wonder the poor woman can't see a way out.

I stroke my sword. "Where can I find these assholes?"

The man barks out a laugh, and I narrow my eyes at him.

Rakiz reaches over and places a leather pouch in the woman's hand. She opens it, and her mouth drops open in shock. She sways on her feet, and the man lunges forward, grabbing her arm. He bares his teeth at Rakiz, and the woman chokes on a sob, tears rolling down her cheeks.

"You...you—" She can't get the words out, but she tries to hand the pouch back.

Rakiz smiles gently and takes her hand. He wraps it around the pouch. "No one deserves such a life," he says. "Tell your sister it is a gift from my tribe to her family."

"May you and your female be blessed for all days," she

says, sobbing as her mate wraps his arm around her, staring at Rakiz and me in shock.

"The same to you," Rakiz says. He nods at the couple, and we turn to walk away.

"Wait," the man says. I turn back, eyes widening as he holds out the dragon scale I admired. The blue is so dark in places that it appears almost black, lightening to an aqua and then finally darkening again to a deep green. It's almost incandescent, gleaming in the light.

I don't know what I would do with a dragon scale, but I clutch it, completely unwilling to give it back.

"Thank you," I say, and the man nods at me before once again wrapping his arm around the woman, who still has tears dripping from her eyes.

I study Rakiz as we walk back through the market. He places his hand at my lower back, scanning for threats as Tagiz walks in front of us, Hewex covering our backs.

Rakiz's upbringing seems to have been the very definition of privileged. He was raised knowing he would rule the tribe, and it's likely that people have been falling over themselves to do his bidding from the moment he could talk.

Even now, I've never seen anyone talk back to him in public. Other than me, of course. I know Terex has disagreed with Rakiz occasionally, but he wouldn't dare question him where others could hear.

Taking all these factors into account, it would be easy to assume that Rakiz would be an entitled prick. A man-child with few skills and fewer morals. At the very least, I wouldn't have been surprised if he was out of touch and unable to empathize with people like the woman who has such a hard life with her sick kids.

And yet...the opposite is true. It's what makes Rakiz such a good ruler. He genuinely cares about people. He wants what's best for them even as he hates the fact that *he* is what's best for his tribe.

A tiny part of my heart fractures as I scan his hard face. For some reason, the reminder that Rakiz is absolutely, one-hundred-percent necessary for the health and well-being of the tribe hurts something deep within me. And I'm not quite sure why.

CHAPTER TEN

R *akiz*

Nevada is quiet while we travel toward the prexa where the human female was last seen. We need to move quickly if we are to get out of the prexas before darkness approaches. While there are few places as dangerous as this area during the day, there are none as dangerous as the prexas at night.

"She will be okay," I murmur, and Nevada snorts.

"You don't know that. What I want to know is how she got separated from the others and how she ended up alone and in the worst part of this planet."

Tagiz moves his mishua level with us. "We must walk to one of the entrances from here," he says, and I nod. It has been many years since I ventured into a prexa, and Tagiz and Hewex now have much more experience in this area.

Nevada swings her legs over the saddle and jumps off, landing in a crouch. She looks like what she is—a dangerous, furious, *sexy* female. Lust hits me in the gut, and I dismount behind her as I force my focus back to the task at hand.

"You will stay close to me the entire time," I tell her, and she turns her head to stare at me with a frown.

"Try that again," she says as she gets to her small feet, tapping one of them.

"I'm not playing games," I tell her. "You will agree to this, or I will tie you to the mishua."

Both Nevada and the mishua in question snort at the same time and then eye each other with distrust.

Nevada scowls at me. "I know you're stressed out, so I'm choosing to overlook the fact that you're once again giving me orders even though I thought we were past this. But since you're obviously in a pissy and slightly unstable mood, I'll tell you that yes, since I have no plans to be killed underground, I'll stay next to you."

She bites out the last three words, and Hewex gives me a look that suggests that I may not be sleeping in Nevada's furs tonight. I suppress a growl and nod instead, turning to gather extra weapons from one of my packs.

I continually war with my urge to dominate this mouthy, intelligent, brave warrior. I know she will make me pay for this conversation later, but I can't risk her life in the prexas without knowing that she will be by my side the entire time.

If anything should happen to her...

I'm almost shaking with tension, and Tagiz steps close as Nevada ensures all her weapons are within easy reach.

"I will protect her with my life," he murmurs, and I nod in gratitude. I recognize that Nevada can more than protect herself, but somehow the knowledge that Tagiz will lay down his life for her if I should fall...

I exhale forcefully and then reach into my final pack,

pulling out the dragon scale. I gesture for Nevada to step closer, and she does, eyebrow raised in challenge.

She yelps as I reach for her shirt and glances around. Both Tagiz and Hewex have found other things to look at, and she turns back to me with a glare.

"What are you doing?"

"Dragon scales are used for many things, but their best use is for armor. There is a reason they are so rare and expensive."

I slide the scale under Nevada's shirt, and she reaches down the front, helping me wiggle it into position. It bends and curves as if part of her skin, and her tight shirt keeps it in place. I step back, nodding approvingly. No swords will be able to slide into her front. I wish I had thought ahead and purchased another for her back.

Nevada's face softens slightly as she gazes up at me.

"I'll be fine," she says. "I won't do anything dumb, I promise. We'll all be fine."

I nod, and within moments we're moving toward the entrance to the prexa. This one is hidden amongst the trees and located between two large boulders. A wooden ladder leads down the hole, and Nevada tenses as we take it in.

"Are you okay?"

She swallows but nods, and Tagiz sends her a sympathetic look.

"It's not as dark as it looks," he tells her. "It's narrow in some places, but the locals cooperate enough to ensure that the passageways are usually lit."

Nevada nods again, sending Tagiz an uneasy smile, and I vow to talk to her about this fear later. I want to know everything about this female—from the things that make her smile to the memories that put shadows in her eyes.

Tagiz smiles back at her reassuringly and then disappears down the hole. I go next, the wood rough under my palms. Hewex will follow after Nevada, ensuring that she is protected.

I hit the dirt floor and watch as Nevada makes her way down.

"I can feel your eyes on my butt," she says, and I grin.

"I'm still a male."

Her boots hit the ground, and she grins up at me. I can't help it; I lean forward and take her mouth.

Tagiz groans. "Shall we get back to our mission?"

Nevada sends Tagiz an easy grin, and he turns as Hewex jumps down beside us. Then we all turn, ready to move deeper into the warren of prexas.

Nevada

I hate it down here.

It smells like piss, vomit, and all kinds of things I'd rather not think about. As we turn the corner, I get a whiff of blood and almost gag at the heady stench. Rakiz steps in front of whatever it is.

"You don't need to see that," he says, face hard as he gestures for me to keep walking.

I almost grin. I've seen any number of disgusting and horrific sights in my twenty-seven years. While I don't need Rakiz to hide them from me, I'm willing to concede that it's a nice gesture.

His order to stay next to him, on the other hand...

I'm willing to give him a break today. He's obviously on edge. Earlier he mentioned that he usually wouldn't dream of sending fewer than ten warriors into this area for any kind of mission. While he's slowly learning that I'm not a fragile flower, today obviously isn't one of the days that he'll be overcoming his natural instincts.

I shiver as the air turns colder. Every twenty feet or so, a lantern burns, providing dim light that I'm incredibly grateful for. Small, tight, enclosed spaces are not my favorite things, and I take a deep breath, suppressing the memories that want to come out and play.

It's not quiet down here. We cross several forks in the path in front of us, and voices reach us. A scream sounds down one passage, and I tense, reaching for my sword. I feel like we're sitting ducks. The space is small enough that it would be difficult for the warriors to fight. But if someone had enough men, they could take us on either side.

A cackling laugh echoes down the prexa, making me flinch, and Rakiz glances back. I nod at him, but I'm sure I look like a deer in headlights.

Of course our best lead to Ivy and the others had to be underground.

Tagiz seems to know where he's going. The plan is simple: head back to the place where Ivy was last seen and slap a few people around until they tell us everything they know.

Another laugh sounds, and it's like ice water down my spine.

"Does anyone down here have a noncreepy laugh?" I mutter.

Hewex snorts behind me. "The laughing is the very least of our concerns."

On that happy note, we head left at the next intersection. This prexa is even more poorly lit than the last one, and I grit my teeth at the sound of shuffling ahead. It pauses and then continues as we get closer.

A lamp goes out somewhere in front of us, and I scowl as the shadows around us grow. This does not bode well. Tagiz keeps moseying down the prexa, and I lovingly caress the hilt of my sword.

We reach a giant as he's extinguishing another lamp. It throws the prexa into even further darkness, and I scowl.

"Dick move, asshole."

I don't know if he's technically a giant, but he would probably stand several feet above the warriors. They've had to bow their heads in places, but this dickhead is walking practically hunched over. He holds out his hand as we get close.

"Fifty credits," he says, and I snort.

Rakiz studies the giant with ice-cold eyes. Like us, the giant's skin is...well...skin-colored. And he has two legs. But that's where the similarities end. I count six arms at first glance, but then the giant turns slightly, showcasing another two sticking out of his back.

His horns look incredibly sharp, and from the pieces of rotting carcass between his huge teeth, it's evident that he's not a vegetarian. One of his hands is wrapped around a huge spiked mace.

"Move or die," Rakiz says, and I nod approvingly. The best threats are simple and to the point.

If I wasn't stuck underground and staring at an eight-armed giant, I'd grin at the dumbstruck look on his face as he stares at Rakiz. I'm guessing most people take one look at his size and immediately pay up.

Rakiz can more than afford to pay the giant, but I've seen this expression before. The lowered brows, narrowed eyes, and—ooh, there it goes—the muscle ticking in his jaw all say one thing and one thing only.

He's more than ready and willing to kill someone.

I lean against the rock and cross my arms. Rakiz has had a rough day. I know every single one of his caveman instincts urged him to leave me safe in the cave or even tied to the mishua as he threatened. He's tired and grumpy, and he feels like he has his back against the wall.

This isn't going to be pretty.

"You die!" the giant roars, and I almost gag at the stench of his breath.

"Jesus, man, you ever thought of using one of those hands to brush your fucking teeth?" I say.

The giant meets my eyes and roars again, and I give him a little finger wave. Best to let Rakiz get this out of his system.

It's messy and brutal. Tagiz is obviously thinking along the same lines as me because he steps aside, letting Rakiz move forward and dispatch the giant.

He starts by cutting off two of the giant's arms.

I stare as both of those arms fall to the ground within a single figure-eight sword stroke. That move was a thing of beauty as Rakiz skillfully dodged the mace when it swung toward his head.

The giant opens his mouth in another roar, and I slap my hands over my ears. His mace hits the wall of the prexa, and I grimace as a tiny waterfall of rocks falls from the roof above us.

The giant swings again, and I tense as Rakiz jumps back. There's hardly any space for him to move. We all scatter to give him more room, but as soon as the mace hits the other wall, Rakiz blocks the fist that's heading toward his face.

With his sword.

"Another one bites the dust," I sing softly to myself as the arm hits the ground. Hewex widens his eyes at me, likely convinced I'm crazy.

I shrug. The enclosed space is definitely getting to me.

The giant lets out a high-pitched shriek, and it's the last sound he ever makes. Rakiz's sword slides through his neck muscles like a knife through butter, and we all watch as what's left of the giant falls to the ground.

Rakiz whips his head around, running his gaze over my body as he checks if I'm okay. I give him a thumbs-up, and he frowns slightly in confusion. His eyes are wild, but he blows out a long breath and sheaths his sword. He nods at Tagiz, who steps over the body, and then Rakiz follows him, waiting on the other side for me.

I frown down. There's no way I can get to the other side without stepping on the giant, and I like these boots. I squeak as Rakiz leans over and lifts me, using nothing but his arms and abs to pull me over the body.

"Show-off," I mutter, but I stroke one hand over his arm in thanks.

The next few minutes are uneventful until we reach yet another crossing. I'm pretty good with directions, but at this point, even I'll struggle to get out of here if our little excursion goes downhill.

We turn left again, following the prexa until we're suddenly standing in a room about the size of the meeting room in Rakiz's hut back at the camp. Five other prexas also lead into this room, all exiting in different directions. This is one of the trading posts that the blue woman told me about.

In fact, there's a blue man who looks a little like the blue woman's mate currently talking to a Voildi. The Voildi sneers at us but says nothing, likely because he's completely outnumbered. The blue man passes something to the Voildi, who hands a small package back, and then the Voildi stalks away, baring his teeth at the warriors.

Tagiz's hand strays to his sword as he contemplates the Voildi.

"No violence in the trading post," a raspy voice says, and I turn, taking in a bent old man. His leathery skin is a shade of blue similar to the alien who just traded with the Voildi, but he's twice the size with numerous horns winding from his head, reminding me of a mishua.

"Seriously?" I ask. "That's a rule?"

He nods. "Neutral ground. Kill someone here, and you'll be hunted by every creature around." The horned man tilts his head at Tagiz, and a slow smile creeps over his face. "Doesn't mean you can't follow him to a quiet prexa and get the job done."

It's clear that Tagiz is itching to go fight the Voildi. He shakes his head though, and the horned man lets out a low laugh.

He's leaning against a large rock, watching the trading happen around us. Rakiz examines the room and reaches behind him, taking the tail of my shirt in his hand and reassuring himself that I'm close.

"Araz," Horned Man says, and the tension level in the trading post shoots sky-high. A few creatures glance at our group and decide they have business elsewhere, scuttling away down various prexas.

"You know who I am," Rakiz says in a silky voice. Horned Man laughs again, and I have the urge to take him by the hand and show him what Rakiz just did to the last creature who pissed him off.

"I do."

The shadow of a smile remains on his mouth, and I sigh.

"How about we cut the crap? What do you want?" I ask.

Horned Man's gaze flicks to me, and he examines me. It's

not sexual, more like he's filing away what I look like for future reference, but Rakiz tenses further.

Horned Man nods suddenly as if deciding something, and he gets to his feet. His face turns serious, and he bows formally to Rakiz.

"You recently helped a friend of mine," he says. "A friend too proud to accept help from those she knows."

Rakiz's face is blank, and Horned Man sighs, his face serious. "You have given her the means to cure her sick children. For the first time, she will be able to get more than a few hours' sleep each night. She will no longer have to listen to the choked sounds of her babies struggling to breathe as she prays to all the gods that she will be able to afford medicine the next day."

My mouth drops open. The expression on his face is... longing. This man cares deeply for that woman. He wants her.

Horned Man's face clears. "You may ask me one question," he says.

Rakiz opens his mouth, and I elbow my way past him, ignoring his low growl.

I stare into Horned Man's eyes. "What do you know about any female women who look similar to me and the places they have been seen on this planet?"

Horned Man smiles at me and nods, satisfaction in his eyes. "There was a female here. She spoke with my friend briefly but didn't linger. She was obviously running from someone. I asked around, and a few others had noticed her appearance as she'd traveled through the prexas. She made it through alive," he says, and I blow out a relieved breath. Something about the way he nods at me tells me that he helped ensure Ivy was as safe as possible.

I open my mouth, but he holds up one hand and continues.

"She entered a prexa in the east, close to Malufic," he says, nodding as Rakiz shifts beside me. "I see you know it. There is just one prexa entrance in this area, so it shouldn't be too difficult to retrace her steps at least to the entrance. After that, you're on your own."

Determination hits me, and I turn to see Rakiz exchanging a look with Hewex.

"What?" I ask.

"I know how to get back to Malufic," Hewex says. "The problem is that we don't have much time before the sun sets. But if we wait until tomorrow, we'll lose even more time."

I glance at Rakiz. "What do you think?"

His face is hard, and I have a feeling I'm not going to like what he says as he opens his mouth. I hold up a hand, panic sliding into me.

"Wait. Just tell me this. How would you do it, if it could be done today?"

Rakiz sighs. "Go straight to Malufic. Ask around, bribe whoever we need to. Locate the other females, since it sounds like Ivy is no longer anywhere near here. Find a safe place to sleep, and then travel back through the prexas in the morning."

"Will the mishua be okay?"

He gives me a look, and I almost laugh. Right. War horses. Or war mishua. Whatever.

"The mishua will be fine. Our safety is questionable," he says, but I can see the light of battle in his eyes. Rakiz craves the challenge. We're surprisingly well matched this way.

"Can we live through it?"

Hewex glances at Rakiz and then meets my eyes. "I have contacts in the area that may provide help. The question you should be asking is whether it is wise for our tribe king to put his safety at risk."

Rakiz stiffens in offense, and I almost roll my eyes. *Good going, Hewex.* Perhaps he really *wants* to go, and this is his backhanded way of making it happen. Either way, implying that Rakiz can't handle himself is a bad move.

"Excuse me for breaking up this scintillating conversation," Horned Man says, and I turn and blink at him. Truthfully, I'd forgotten he was there. "But by now, that Voildi will have spread the word that there are three Braxians traveling alone in this area. You would be smart to make a decision and leave."

Rakiz looks at me, and I try to keep myself from pleading with my expression. If he truly believes we're all going to end up dead today, I'll accept it and we can come back tomorrow. We're no use to the other women if we're murdered before we can get to them.

"Is Inexa still in Malufic, Hewex?" he asks, his gaze steady on my face.

Tagiz clears his throat, shifting on his feet. I glance at him, and he looks away as he nods. Whoever this Inexa person is, they've got Tagiz nervous.

A muscle twitches in Rakiz's cheek. "Let's go. Now."

CHAPTER ELEVEN

N *evada*

THE GUYS ARE TENSE AS WE TRAVEL THROUGH THE PREXAS, and no one speaks. Tagiz seems to know his way around this place the best, and he takes the lead once we've left the trading post behind.

The confined space and darkness are getting to me. At one point, I hear a voice murmuring, and my mind turns it into Arabic. Just like that I'm in Baghdad, wondering if I'll ever see the sky, ever breathe fresh air, ever feel the sun on my skin again.

Rakiz seems to feel my tension, and he leans closer at one point, brushing a kiss over my temple. I manage to keep my heart from melting, but it's a close call.

Tagiz sniffs at one point. "Voildi," he growls.

We don't have the time for another fight, and Tagiz's huge body is trembling with tension as he gestures to a prexa that will take us slightly off our planned route.

Finally we're close to the exit. I think I've gone slightly nose blind, but the first whiff of fresh air is a welcome relief, and my shoulders relax as the prexa slowly lightens and we arrive at another ladder.

Tagiz pauses while halfway up, his head sticking out slightly as he scans our surroundings. He nods, and Rakiz climbs up behind him, gesturing for me to follow him. I'm not surprised when Rakiz's strong arms grab me and pull me up once I'm on the ladder.

We're in another forest, but I can see small buildings through the trees.

Buildings.

I frown. I assumed that everyone here lived in kradis or similar tents.

I voice my thought, and a grin transforms Hewex's face.

"Our tribe is nomadic," he says, "but that does not mean that everyone on this planet lives the same way. Even Dexar's tribe returns to their kingdom during the cold season."

Wow.

The buildings are tiny and squat, practically falling apart. I've seen slums that looked more welcoming, and with the warriors so tense from the constant danger, it's easy to see why this area is mostly avoided.

We don't hang around, and I bask in the fresh air, enjoying the weak late-afternoon sun on my face while we follow Tagiz. Rakiz seems to get tenser as we get closer to the buildings, and I study his face when he glances at me.

He opens his mouth as if to say something and then snaps it shut, scowling into the distance. Whatever is going on with him will have to wait because Tagiz is walking at a brisk pace. We stay under the cover of the trees as we move closer to the buildings, traveling behind them until Tagiz seems to find one he recognizes.

"Seriously," I mutter to Rakiz. "What's up?"

He simply shakes his head, and Tagiz glances at us.

"Wait here," he says and then darts forward to what looks like a tiny house. He knocks on the door, and I can't see who opens it, but they have a brief conversation before the stranger opens the door further, stepping into view.

I inhale sharply. The woman is Braxian, and one look at Rakiz's face tells me that he knows her well.

She glances at the trees where we're waiting and then nods once at Tagiz, her face hard. He leads her back to us, and only an idiot wouldn't see the red flags as she looks at Rakiz.

These two have history.

"Inexa," Rakiz says, and she nods, not taking her eyes off his face. It's as if she's dying of thirst and he's holding out a waterskin.

"It has been a long time," she says softly.

It's obvious that this woman has had a hard life. She's beautiful, with dark hair that, while no longer shiny, is thick and long. She's thinner than any Braxian woman I've ever seen, but if she's living alone here, that could be due to malnutrition.

Her dark-brown eyes are luminous, and while the line between her brows speaks of pain, I'm guessing she'd be gorgeous if she smiled.

Who is she to Rakiz?

"It has," Rakiz says, and I force myself to focus on the present.

She smiles at him, and I was right. Her smile transforms her. Then she turns to me, her gaze scanning me curiously.

"We need your help," Tagiz says quietly, and Inexa glances at him before returning her attention to Rakiz.

I know that look. And Rakiz's tension suddenly makes a lot more sense. These two have been lovers. I don't know why she's not part of the tribe, but from the look in her eyes, Inexa still considers Rakiz to be hers.

Thanks for the heads-up, Rakiz.

"You know I will help you any way I can," Inexa says, her voice low, and Rakiz nods, a muscle pulsing in his jaw as he looks at me.

Oh yes, we'll be talking about this little situation, my warrior and I.

Hewex steps forward and explains what we need.

Inexa nods. "Yes, I heard of these women. One of them escaped, and a pack of Voildi went door-to-door, searching our homes." Inexa glances at me as if I'm the one to blame for this, and I barely refrain from rolling my eyes.

I open my mouth to question her but snap it shut when Tagiz glances at me. Yep, I should definitely leave the asking to Rakiz.

Rakiz smiles at Inexa, but it doesn't reach his eyes. "I'm sorry to hear of your troubles," he says. "What can you tell us of where we can find these women?"

Inexa's eyes widen. "There are rumors that they're being kept close by until they're sold. A new pack of Voildi moved into the area a few months ago, and they have taken over several of the houses on the eastern side of the village. They ran the owners out of their homes."

The more I learn about these Voildi, the more certain I am that they need to die. Unfortunately, we don't have enough of us to take on a giant pack of Voildi and rescue the other women at the same time. This mission is going to have to rely on stealth.

"Can you give us directions to this place?" Rakiz asks, and Inexa nods.

"It's too dangerous around here after dark," she says. "What is your plan?"

Rakiz and Tagiz share a look, and I have a feeling that they're silently communicating about whether they can trust Inexa.

"We will find a place close by and then will return through the prexas tomorrow."

Inexa immediately shakes her head. "If you manage to steal the females, the Voildi will tear the forest apart looking for them. They will expect you to stay close to the prexa, and there are more of them than you can imagine."

Rakiz grinds his teeth.

"What do you suggest?" I ask, no longer willing to be silent.

Inexa glances at me. "You can stay with me," she says. "My home is humble, but after the first female escaped, the Voildi will not imagine that any of us would dare hide anyone from them."

Her eyes are suddenly haunted, and I stroke my sword as I imagine just how the Voildi managed to instill that sense of fear.

They're monsters who prey on the weak. And those who prey on the weak should be taught a lesson they won't forget.

I'm almost shaking as I imagine burning their lair to the ground and making them pay. Hewex nudges me, and I blink, forcing myself to focus again.

"We're ready to go," Hewex says, and I nod. Inexa returns to her home, and we skulk through the forest until we're close to the Voildi's base. From the looks on the warriors' faces, the smell is enough to confirm that the Voildi are close and we're in the right place.

We hunker down and watch. The Voildi have taken a few houses and probably knocked down walls to turn them into a larger lair. Voildi come and go, with no signs of the human women. At one point, a large furry male appears, striding into the lair. He's shorter than the warriors but twice as wide, and his claws are so long that I gulp.

The Voildi allow him to pass, and his roar sounds a few minutes later.

"Where is the flame-haired one? I told you I wanted *her*."

Whatever the Voildi say obviously doesn't please the creature because he roars again, striding out of the lair. Any Voildi dumb enough to get in his way soon regrets it, and he picks one of them up, throwing him toward the forest. The Voildi hits a tree, his neck breaking with a snap.

The next Voildi is gutted with the male's claws, and the Voildi after that is obviously an idiot because he dares to pull a weapon.

He's dispatched in the blink of an eye, and then the furred male strides back through the village.

Well, shit.

Voildi rush from the lair, staring at their fallen pack members. One of them is obviously the leader because the others quickly move out of his way when he stalks out, taking in the bodies.

He's wearing an eye patch, and his face turns a darker yellow as it contorts in rage. "Why hasn't that flame-haired whore been found yet?" he screams, and the Voildi all remain silent.

This seems to enrage him further.

"What are you doing here? Why aren't you out looking for the bitch? She took my fucking eye!"

My grin is so wide that my cheeks begin to hurt, and Hewex sends me a look.

"Human females," he murmurs. "As vicious as they are lovely."

One of the Voildi steps forward. "We-We are hunting her, milord."

The leader hauls back and kicks the body at his feet, and I almost gag as entrails sprawl onto the ground.

"Enough," he says. "I grow tired of having so much of the pack lying around here. There is no need for so many to be guarding one female. I want six males to join the hunt today."

"But milord—"

"Do you challenge me?"

"No milord."

The leader turns and walks inside, leaving the other Voildi to collect the bodies.

I turn to Rakiz, and he gestures for us to fall back further into the cover of the trees.

"Did you hear that?" I whisper. "There's only one female left here."

Rakiz nods. "We will wait until the hunting party has left. Even six fewer Voildi will make our task easier."

I blow out a breath, forcing myself to push away my anxiety about the two other women for now. "We need a distraction. Something to make the Voildi all rush to the front of the lair again."

Hewex grins at me while Rakiz scowls.

"Don't say it."

"I'm the obvious choice," I continue, ignoring him. "I can borrow a dress from Inexa and pretend to be a helpless female who's just looking for her missing friend. You guys sneak in the back and find whoever's left, and then we can haul ass out of here."

Okay, so there are a few holes in that plan.

Rakiz's brow lowers even further, and he opens his mouth even as Tagiz shakes his head.

"How would you get away from all those Voildi?"

I examine the lair. The more I look at it, the more I can see the signs that they've knocked down walls. But something tells me that they didn't consult the Agron version of an architect before they did it.

"That lair doesn't look all that stable. Looks like it wouldn't take much for the whole thing to come crashing down."

Rakiz eyes me, but he turns, and we all look at the buildings.

"If only we had some explosives," I murmur, and Hewex tilts his head.

"Explosives." He repeats the word in English, and I realize there's no translation.

"Yeah." I explain what they do, and Tagiz leans against a tree, meeting Hewex's eyes.

"We may be able to find something that would work," he says.

"What? Really?"

Rakiz is still obviously in a pissy mood, but he reaches out an arm and pulls me close. "I like the way you are thinking except for the part where you use yourself as bait. That will never happen while I still have breath in my body."

I roll my eyes. "I'm the obvious choice."

He ignores me, but he knows I'm right.

CHAPTER TWELVE

R *akiz*

To say that I'm unhappy with this plan is an understatement.

The thought of putting Nevada in danger...it makes me want to throw her over my shoulder and haul her back to my camp.

I glance at Tagiz and Hewex. We've moved deeper into the forest while they search for the Trelga tree pods. They're difficult to find, but they appear in bunches, so if we can locate one bunch, we will have more than enough for our needs.

"I still don't get what we're doing," Nevada says.

"You will see."

She has been quiet ever since she met Inexa. I want to explain to her who Inexa is and why she lives here instead of in my camp where she should be settled with a mate. But now is not the time.

Nevada is choosing to leave this conversation for later; however, I'm not fooled into thinking she will forget about it.

She's currently pacing back and forth while Tagiz and Hewex examine a large tree. Unlike those in the Seinex Forest, the trees here are made of a deep-blue bark with large green leaves.

Tagiz jumps and hauls himself onto a branch before climbing until he gets near the top of the tree.

"Jeez," Nevada says. "He climbs like a monkey."

I don't enjoy her appreciating any other males, and I reach out, pulling her close. I press a kiss beneath her jaw, and she smiles at me, although it doesn't reach her eyes.

Tagiz is back on the ground within moments, a branch covered in pods clutched in his hand.

Hewex lets out a low whoop, his eyes dancing, and Nevada laughs.

"How do they work?"

"We need fire," Tagiz says. "Once these pods are set aflame, they will cause the damage you described."

"An explosion," Nevada says, and her voice is excited. "Excellent."

We take the pods back to Inexa's small home, and I can tell by the way she avoids my eyes that she is shamed to have us here. And yet she has opened her door to us to keep us safe. I will not forget it, and I vow to once more attempt to convince her to return to camp with us.

I explain our plan to Inexa, and her eyes widen as she glances at Nevada.

"It is very dangerous," she says, and Nevada shrugs.

"As I've already explained to Rakiz, they're not going to kill me. They need more human females to sell, especially since they're currently down two. I'll only be with them for a moment while I distract them, and then they'll be too busy trying not to die to bother with me."

I grind my teeth, and Inexa's gaze lands on my face. She gives me a knowing look, and her face creases in pain for a single moment. I have not touched Nevada in front of her—have barely looked at her or spoken to her—yet somehow Inexa knows exactly how I feel about her.

"Would you happen to have a dress I can borrow?" Nevada asks, and Inexa examines her form.

"It will be too big."

"I know. But they won't be paying much attention, and I just need to look less like myself... More...helpless.

Nevada seems to realize what she's just said, because a flush travels up her cheekbones. "I didn't mean—"

"I know," Inexa says, her smile serene, and Nevada hunches her shoulders. Inexa's gaze scans Nevada's body, traveling from her leather pants to her vest and lingering on the gold band circling her upper arm. Inexa glances at me and then quickly looks away, moving into her small bedroom. She comes back with a blue dress, and Nevada smiles at her awkwardly before pulling it on over her clothes.

The dress drags on the ground, and it's definitely too large. Inexa reaches over and helps her tighten the strings at the back, ensuring that it won't fall down.

"Well," Nevada says, "what do you think?"

Hewex snorts. "You look like a mishua wearing Braxian clothes," he says.

Nevada scowls but bites her lip with suppressed laughter. I send Hewex a look, and then Nevada raises her eyebrow in challenge as she meets my gaze.

"You look fine, karja," I say.

She smiles at me, her eyes inviting me to share the joke,

and for a moment the rest of the world disappears as I stare at my warrior female.

Inexa moves back, her eyes suddenly blank, and I almost curse. I am not trying to hurt her, and I send her a glance of apology as Nevada narrows her eyes at me.

"Okay," Nevada says finally, breaking the awkward silence. "Let's get this done."

We move back through the forest and toward the Voildi's lair. They've removed the bodies, and a group are standing outside, waiting to depart.

"Bring me the flame-haired female," the leader says. "If you fail in this, I will make you wish you had never been born."

"Not a bad threat," Nevada murmurs beside me. "It would probably have more weight to it if the *'flame-haired female'* wasn't responsible for the sissy eye patch he's wearing."

Tagiz grins beside me, and we watch as the Voildi depart. They're moving back through the village, likely toward the prexa. Once they've gone, we crouch behind a large bush.

I grind my teeth, and Nevada reaches out, stroking her hand down my jaw. "It'll be okay," she says quietly. "I promise."

"You can't promise that." My voice is hoarse, and Tagiz and Hewex look away, giving us a thin illusion of privacy.

"I trust you guys to have my back. It's a good plan, Rakiz."

I disagree. Any plan that puts my stubborn female at risk is not a good plan. But she's right about one thing—it's the only plan that makes sense. If a Braxian warrior were to approach the Voildi lair, the creatures would immediately go into defense mode. The human female would also be locked down and immediately surrounded.

The Voildi won't see Nevada as a threat, a fact that she's counting on. Her presence will create enough of a diversion that we can rescue the other female and make these Voildi pay for their actions.

But I don't have to like it.

Nevada hands me her sword. She has knives tucked into her boots but can't risk appearing as a threat in any way.

"Look after this for me," she says. "I'll want it right back."

I reach out and pull her to me, swallowing her gasp as I plunder her mouth. We're running out of time, but I need to feel her soft lips under mine before I allow her to risk her safety.

Her hand comes up, stroking my face, and I feel some of the tension leave my body. I trust that Nevada can protect herself, and I believe in my warriors. And if the Voildi harm a single hair on my female's head, I'll make them wish they had never been born.

Nevada's eyes are bright as she moves back. "Help me out with this, Jack," she whispers to the sky.

Then, with a single glance at us, she's gone, moving back through the forest so she can approach the Voildi from the village.

Hewex and Tagiz disappear, and I clench my jaw until it feels as if my teeth will crack. I can't join Nevada until she has lured most of the Voildi from their lair. But I move close enough that if they attempt to hurt her, I can be next to her within moments.

There are two Voildi stationed outside the exit, and one of them raises his voice in excitement as he suddenly turns his head, calling to those inside. Nevada appears, and I curl my hands into fists as I force myself to allow her to play her part.

She has blood and dirt on her face, and I scowl as I realize she's obviously cut herself somewhere in an effort to appear more vulnerable. Twigs and dirt are embedded in her hair, and a shallow wound on her neck seeps blood.

Oh, we will talk, my female warrior and I.

She walks with a limp, freezing as the Voildi step in front of her.

"Human female," one of them says, voice shocked.

"Please," Nevada says, her voice wavering. "I need to speak to whoever's in charge."

More Voildi appear, grins on their faces, and Nevada trembles, taking a step back. Blood drips into my palms as my fingernails dig into them with the effort required to hold myself back.

The leader appears, pushing Voildi out of the way until he stares at Nevada. A slow smile spreads over his face, and she tilts her head. Anyone who didn't know Nevada would assume she is frightened, but I've seen that cold, cunning gaze each time she has sized up an enemy.

"Female," the Voildi says, "why have you come here?"

Nevada visibly gulps, holding her hands out from her body and drawing attention to the fact that she's unarmed. "I've come for my friends," she says. "I know you have them here."

The leader lets out a laugh, and the other Voildi echo him. More of them appear from within the lair, obviously curious to see what is so amusing.

"You were stupid to come here," the leader says. "But I will benefit from your stupidity. You can see your friends. In fact, you will have more time with them than you could have imagined before I sell you to the highest bidder."

Nevada backs away a step, her head twisting from side to side. The leader grins, moving closer, and I turn at a rustle in the trees close by.

Tagiz appears behind me, a human female clutched tightly in his arms. Her face is pale, and it appears as if she is struggling to breathe. He places her down and leans her against a tree before creeping closer.

Now we wait.

A Voildi runs outside from within the lair, the yellow color leaching from his face as he shoves his way forward.

"Milord—"

"Not now."

"But milord—"

The leader ignores him, and Nevada smiles.

"Nice eye patch," she says. "You look like Captain Hook and a jaundiced frog had a baby."

The Voildi steps forward, his smile fading as he bares his teeth at Nevada. Whatever reference she has just made, it's obvious that it's an insult, and the Voildi narrows his eye at her.

"Milord—"

"What's the matter?" she asks, speaking over the pale Voildi, who is now trembling as he attempts to get his leader's attention. "Cat got your eye? Oh right...that was my friend, wasn't it? Tell me, did it hurt when a *female* disfigured you? Ooh...that's embarrassing."

"I'll take your eye as payment," the Voildi hisses, stepping closer, and Nevada smiles at him.

"Milord! The human female—she's gone!"

The leader's mouth drops open, and he growls at Nevada's satisfied grin.

"Take her," he orders the two Voildi closer to Nevada, and then he stalks back inside the lair. Most of the Voildi follow, and I finally jolt forward, my body shaking with the need to spill blood.

"Oh, hey, baby," Nevada says as I reach her. She grins at me as she takes her sword from hand. "I was wondering when you'd turn up."

Her tone is lightly teasing, and it soothes something inside me.

The Voildi charge, and I behead two of them with one blow. Nevada darts away, quick as lightening as she dodges a Voildi who is still attempting to take her alive. She knees him in the balls, her sword sliding into his chest as he bends, and I dispatch any others who think to come close.

BOOM!

The roof of the lair blows off, fire sweeping through the building, and I pull Nevada away as the last Voildi's gaze darts between us and the building, and he runs into the forest, where Tagiz is waiting.

"You got her out, right?" Nevada asks, and I nod, pulling her back toward the forest. I don't know how many Voildi will have survived, but we need to disappear. Now.

"That was fun," Nevada murmurs, and I feel the corner of my mouth curl.

"Insane female," I say, and she grins up at me.

***

Nevada

Zoey is slumped against a tree, and my triumph immediately transforms into worry as I crouch next to her. She opens her eyes and gives me a tiny smile.

"Nevada, right?"

I nod. "Are you okay?"

"I knew someone would come for me," she whispers, ignoring my question. Then her whole body shakes as she coughs, groaning in pain as she gasps for breath.

She's covered in dirt, her hair a tangled mess. One of her arms cradles her side, and I glance up at Tagiz as he kneels next to me.

"Zoey was kicked in the ribs by one of the aliens who bought us," I tell him. "I'm guessing they haven't healed much."

His face is grim, and he leans close to Zoey, who studies him with tired eyes. Her breathing is shallow, and her face is so pale she looks gray. I place the back of my hand against her forehead and curse.

She's burning up.

"You're sick," I say, stating the obvious.

"I'm a nurse," she says. "That first alien broke my ribs. I'm pretty sure I've got pneumonia now. I'm guessing you don't have any antibiotics on you?"

She coughs again, and Tagiz's eyes are wild as they meet mine.

"Antibiotics aren't really a thing here," I say, and she smiles weakly.

"I didn't think so," she murmurs. "Hey, at least I'm outside now. I was certain I'd die in that shithole."

Tagiz lets out a low growl. "You're not dying, female."

I almost tell him not to make promises he can't keep. Pneumonia is serious. I get to my feet and move to where Rakiz and Hewex are talking quietly.

"If we don't get her to a healer, she's dead," I say, and my voice cracks on the last word. Rakiz reaches for me, and I step away. I don't have time to break down.

"What's wrong with her?" he asks.

"Broken rib, constantly being moved, poor nutrition, and no drugs. She's sick as a dog."

Rakiz nods and gestures at Tagiz, who leans down, gently picking up Zoey as her face tenses in pain.

"I'm sorry, female," he murmurs, and she nods, resting her head against his chest.

"Let's go," Rakiz says, and we move back to Inexa's home. As much as I want to head straight back to camp so Zoey can see the healers, it's already getting dark, and we can't risk traveling through the prexas at night. Zoey needs to be carried, which means Tagiz won't have his hands free.

We'd be sitting ducks for anyone looking for us.

Inexa's face is pale when she answers the door, and the relief is clear on her face when she scans Rakiz's body and finds him uninjured. We file in, and I peel out of the long, heavy dress, feeling like a weight has been lifted off my shoulders.

We still need to find Ivy, Beth, and Charlie, but at least we've saved Zoey from those Voildi assholes. Rage makes my hands shake as Tagiz gently lays her down, close to the tiny window. They've almost killed her.

I crouch next to her, wincing at her shallow breaths. "How are you doing, girl?"

She blinks up at me, a hint of a smile curling her lips. "Peachy."

The warriors huddle together, likely making backup plans for their backup plans, and Inexa moves close, a small bucket in her hand.

She places it down and hands me a cloth, and I smile at her gratefully. Zoey lets out a moan as I wipe her face before rinsing the cloth.

"God, that feels good," she says. "I must stink."

"You should've seen me when I finally bathed back at the camp," I say. "It was seriously gross."

Rakiz moves closer and nods. "She's right," he says. "I almost had to kick her out of my tashiv."

Zoey grins at him, and I see a hint of the woman she was on Earth.

"What can you tell me?" I murmur, frowning as I take in her torn pajamas. After the way the Voildi treated her, I'm not sure why I'm shocked that she wasn't given a change of clothes, but it pisses me off.

I hope they hurt as they died.

"We had a deal," she murmurs softly. Inexa offers her some water, and she sips at it with a sigh. "Ivy, Beth, and I. If there was a chance for one of us to get away, we would. None of us wanted to leave the others behind, but we knew it was our best chance.

"They were planning to sell us at a slave market, and they lost their minds when they found out it had been destroyed. Beth had managed to convince them that she was weak and slightly stupid. She saw her chance and took off."

Zoey blinks back tears, and I take her hand. I can't imagine what it was like for both of them. It must've killed Beth to leave, but it would've been just as bad to be the one left behind.

"She never came back," Zoey says, a choked sob leaving her. "I know she would've returned if she could. She didn't want to go, but Ivy made her. Something happened to Beth. Something terrible."

Shit.

I glance at Rakiz, and his face is hard.

"And Ivy?" I ask.

"After Beth disappeared, we were separated. I don't

know where she was taken, but she put up one hell of a fight."

"She got free," I tell her. "She was last seen escaping through the prexas—underground tunnels. Wherever she is, we'll find her. Beth too."

Zoey nods, but any energy she had seems to have left her. Her eyes are sliding closed, but Tagiz kneels next to us.

"You must eat, female," he says to her. "You need your strength."

She studies his face and then finally nods, taking the dried meat he hands her. She nibbles it, but I can see she has no appetite.

Rakiz draws me to my feet and pulls me aside.

"We need to get back to the camp as soon as possible," I say, and he nods.

"If I thought we could make it tonight, we would go. But the risk is too high."

"I know."

He offers me some dried meat, scowling at me until I take it. I'm not hungry either, but I know it's important that we keep our strength up.

Inexa finds a few blankets, and Rakiz and I lie on the ground. At one point, screams sound from somewhere in the village, and the tension shoots up.

Inexa peeks out the window. "If there are any Voildi left, they will be hunting you," she murmurs.

"If they come close, we will leave and take our chances," Rakiz says from next to me. I coax Zoey into drinking some more water and then curl up as Rakiz moves closer, sliding his arm around me.

Inexa nods absently, still staring out the window. Then she casts one last look at Rakiz and moves into her bedroom, shutting the door behind her.

We're taking turns on watch tonight. Hewex is going first, followed by Rakiz, then Tagiz, and then me.

Hewex is currently outside in the forest, keeping an eye on the house and surrounding area.

"Are you going to tell me what's going on between you and Inexa?" I ask finally, and Rakiz shakes his head.

He reaches out his arm and pulls me close.

"Tomorrow," he says, and I sigh but rest my head on his chest and close my eyes.

CHAPTER THIRTEEN

R *akiz*

MY EYES FLY OPEN, AND I REACH FOR MY KNIFE AS NEVADA cries out in her sleep. I scan our surroundings, and she lets out a sound that I never want to hear again. One full of sadness and suffering. If agony had a sound, it would be the groan ripped from Nevada's throat.

Hewex is sitting up, wrapped in a blanket, likely unwilling to sleep. Tagiz is on watch outside, and thanks to Nevada's insistence, she'll trade with him. She doesn't know yet, but I'll be staying on watch with her.

Hewex glances at Nevada, pity on his face. I'm glad she can't see his expression right now because she would likely reach for her sword.

The stubborn female is proud.

Hewex seems to realize this because he wraps his blanket closer around himself and heads outside, giving us privacy.

Nevada chokes on a sob, and I can't stand it anymore. I lean over and take her mouth, feeling her tense as she wakes beneath me.

I run my hand over her face, which is wet from tears, and move back as Nevada bats my hand away and sits up.

"I was crying," she says, voice flat. "Did I yell out?"

Her gaze flicks to where Hewex was sleeping and lingers on Zoey's still form before her eyes narrow on me.

I won't lie. I nod, and her gaze goes blank as she stares at the wall.

"I knew I'd dream. The moment I saw that hole in the ground at the entrance to the prexa, I knew," she murmurs, shaking her head. "The weirdest things bring it all back."

"Talk to me," I say in a tone that's perilously close to begging.

She sighs, shaking her head, and I take her hand.

"Please."

Nevada shrugs and then sighs again as she meets my eyes. "You know, it's strange what the brain does when you're held captive. Some days, you're certain you'll be going home. Others, you're positive that you'll die there, far from home and surrounded by enemies. It was kind of ironic, really. The girl who kept running away from school because she had problems with authority was forced to rely on her captors for everything—from getting enough to eat to going to the bathroom. Some days, I'd lie curled in a ball for hours. Other days, I'd pick fights with the guards. Stupid, I know."

I lean over and rub my nose against hers, bringing a tiny smile to her mouth, although it doesn't reach her eyes.

"Strangely this doesn't surprise me."

The thought of this small female trapped far from home and surrounded by those who want to kill her, those who tortured her and brought shadows to her emerald eyes...it makes me want to roar.

I run my finger over her face, so incredibly glad that she was freed. "You once told me that you were a warrior. I didn't believe you," I say. "I'm sorry."

She shrugs. "Now that I've been on this planet for as long as I have, I can see why it would be hard for you to believe. Women don't fight here. They don't dress the way I do. Of course you were shocked."

"I still should not have doubted you. You are a brave female. I'm proud of you, even when the things you do turn my bowels to water."

She smiles at me and then rolls to her feet. "I'm not going to get back to sleep. I may as well take over from Tagiz. You should get some sleep before it's your turn."

I sigh as I watch her leave, wishing I could take away the memories that make her cry.

Nevada

Tagiz insists on staying on watch, and even my blackest look can't shake him.

"I won't sleep," he says.

"Neither will I."

"I will," Hewex's voice makes me jump, and his low laugh sounds as he moves back toward the small house.

I scowl and leave Tagiz to his spot, moving closer to the house but still not close enough to be visible from anyone walking nearby. I sit for an hour or so, attempting to shake off the nightmare, and then I'm narrowing my eyes as Inexa comes out of the house.

Her eyes go straight to the bush I'm hiding behind, and I scowl.

"What gave me away?" I ask, and she gives me a confused look. "You knew I was here."

"Oh. The moonlight glinted off one of your knives."

I raise my eyebrow, impressed. I have a knife clutched in my hand, and I place it on the ground.

"The stars are so different here," I murmur, and she lets out a low laugh, studying the sky as she sits next to me.

"I can only imagine."

She seems content to sit in silence, but I've never been known to leave things well enough alone.

"Why don't you live back at camp?"

Inexa keeps her eyes on the sky. "I used to. I left because it was easier."

"Easier than what?"

"Easier than watching Rakiz choose a queen who wouldn't be me."

My mouth falls open, but she's still staring at the stars as if she hasn't just dropped a bomb of epic proportions.

"I figured you guys were together at one point. What happened? Did you break up?"

She smiles slightly, but there's nothing happy in that smile. "When I was young, I was in much demand by the males. I enjoyed it—the attention. I loved how they would fight over me, challenge each other, attempt to find their way into my affections."

"Rakiz was one of those males."

She slowly shakes her head. "Not at first. He had every single female vying for his attention. I wanted him, but I knew if I was to compete for our future king, I would have to be different. Whenever he was in camp, I made sure to always be where he was, but I never paid him any attention.

Rakiz loves a challenge." Inexa glances at me and nods at whatever she sees on my face. "I see you know this."

I swallow around the sudden lump in my throat. "You were a challenge."

She nods, turning her gaze back to the sky. "Eventually I let him win me. But I was stupid, you see. I fell in love."

"Why was that stupid?"

"Because Rakiz was to be king. He couldn't pick a mate who had enjoyed so many males. He couldn't have someone who was gossiped about—someone who would damage his reputation."

"He said that to you?" My outrage is clear even in my whisper.

She shrugs. "He didn't have to. It was always supposed to be a fling, you see. He was barely even at camp, but eventually the whispers began. He'd been with me longer than any other female, and his father was making noises about him finding a mate. A mate that wasn't me."

"That's so unfair."

Inexa turns her whole body, her gaze frank. "It's unfair, but it's life. One day, Rakiz will take a queen. A queen that is well-mannered, popular among the tribe, and ready to bear him heirs. She will sit by his side and smile at his people and be his perfect match in every way."

I don't think Inexa is trying to be cruel, but it feels like I've been stabbed in the gut. I actually gasp out loud, and her expression turns sympathetic.

"You understand. Rakiz had slowly begun to pull away. He was away from camp more than he was in it, and my insecurities made things worse. Every time he spoke to a female who wasn't me...let's just say it was evident that we wouldn't be together for much longer. If I hadn't fallen in love with him, I could have moved on. I could have found a mate and stayed in the tribe, had children, and lived my life."

"But you'd fallen in love," I murmur, and she nods.

"I had. I couldn't sit by and watch as he fell in love with a woman who wasn't me. A woman who would rule with him and bear his children and wake up next to him every day."

"So you left."

"Yes."

"Why didn't you go join another tribe? They're all crying out for females, right?"

She shrugs. "The tribe kings occasionally work together. There was a high chance I would still see Rakiz and his future queen another time. I wanted to be alone."

"And then we knocked on your door."

She gives me a tired smile. "And then you knocked on my door."

Nevada

We leave before dawn, reaching the entrance to the prexa as the sun rises.

Rakiz shared a long look with Inexa when we left.

"I thank you for your hospitality," he said formally, and she simply nodded, her heart in her eyes as she closed the door.

Her words have played on repeat in my head since she spoke them. As a result, I'm so tired I feel nauseous and even more irritable than ever.

Rakiz leads the way through the prexas. I follow behind him, Tagiz carries Zoey in his arms, and Hewex brings up the rear. Zoey is mostly asleep, and I find myself continually glancing back to check that she's still breathing.

Tagiz meets my eyes at one point and jerks his head to where he's resting one finger close to Zoey's mouth and nose.

He'll notice if she stops breathing.

This trip through the prexas is thankfully less eventful than the last. The giant's body has been removed, and I let out a sigh of relief when we finally climb out of the prexas and find the mishua waiting.

Hewex takes Zoey and then passes her up to Tagiz. We stop by the cave to pick up the supplies we left behind and then keep moving.

We can't risk riding too fast. Any jostling could be seriously bad for Zoey. If her ribs are broken in multiple places, a shard could puncture her lung or another organ. For that reason, we stick to a fast walk, and Tagiz holds her carefully in his arms.

She still hasn't woken back up.

"She will be okay, Nevada."

Rakiz's voice is low in my ear, and I glance back at him.

"How do you know that?"

"Human females are strong. After everything that the Voildi put Zoey through, she will not allow this to kill her."

I like his positive thinking, but I'm not sure he knows how pneumonia works.

"My brother had broken ribs once," I say. "One of my mother's boyfriend's beat the shit out of him. He could barely stand and ended up in the emergency room."

Tagiz glances at me, and I shut my mouth. He's taken care of Zoey since we found her, and from the look on his face, he doesn't want to hear about how badly she's injured.

I sigh and lean back against Rakiz. "I just realized I've never asked. Do you have any siblings?"

I feel him shake his head behind me.

"My mother died in childbirth when I'd seen five summers. Braxian babies are large, and births require the attendance of the healer to ensure the pelvis widens enough. The baby was incorrectly positioned, and my mother decided to go for a walk near a river. She went into labor alone with no one but her servants close by. One of them ran back to camp for help, but by the time my father arrived with the healers, it was too late."

There's a common theme here. First, both of his parents were as stubborn as Rakiz, and second, both of them died in circumstances that could have been prevented. No wonder he's so overprotective of anyone he considers under his command.

"That must have been so hard," I murmur.

"Yes. I may never have wanted to rule, but the first thing my father taught me was that a good ruler puts the wants and needs of his tribe ahead of himself. I may not have wanted to be king, but I'm a good king."

"No one else could do it?"

He shrugs. "By the time my father died, I had seen tribes fall. I'd seen women raped and murdered, good warriors castrated, tortured, and left to die. I'd heard of children ripped from their mothers' arms and taken to be slaves. The tribe responsible for these atrocities fell to Dexar's warriors ten summers ago, but that does not mean that the same couldn't happen again. What is my happiness compared to the safety and security of the men, women, and children in my tribe?"

I nod. I get it. It's not fair, but I get it. But it hurts, somewhere deep inside me, to see how different Rakiz is away from the camp.

I push that thought away. It's a good thing that I won't be seeing this side of Rakiz for much longer. The imperious, arrogant king who goes toe to toe with me back at the camp? He's sexy as hell, even if I've never admitted it to myself. But the funny, overprotective, quick-to-laugh Rakiz I see out here in the wild?

I could fall for this Rakiz if I'm not careful. And this Rakiz is only temporary.

The other Rakiz? He's a tribe king who will eventually take a queen.

"A queen that is well-mannered, popular among the tribe, and ready to bear him heirs. She will sit by his side and smile at his people and be his perfect match in every way."

I almost flinch, and Rakiz pulls me closer.

"What's wrong?"

"Nothing," I say. "Nothing at all."

CHAPTER FOURTEEN

N*evada*

It took us three days to get back to camp.

I hadn't realized how fast we'd traveled on the way there, but with Zoey in such poor condition, we had to continually stop to make sure she was hydrated. I wished for a car, bargaining with any god that was listening to keep Zoey alive.

Moni took one look at Zoey and inhaled so sharply she choked. Then she ordered everyone who wasn't a healer to leave the tent. I frowned at her, and she simply narrowed her eyes and waited me out.

Tagiz refused to leave, and Moni eventually threw her hands up in the air.

"Fine. You will hold her down. This will not be pleasant. For anyone."

I stepped forward, but Rakiz wrapped his arm around me.

"Come, karja," he said. "Leave the healers to their work. Zoey will need you when she wakes, which means you must take care of yourself while she is in good hands."

Now I'm sitting in the bath while Rakiz washes me, his hands smoothing soap over my skin. He lets out a pleased sound as he works some of the knots out of my neck, and I sigh.

"I want you to promise you will not go after the other two women without me," he rumbles, and I can practically feel those knots reforming as my muscles tense.

"I don't know if I can make that promise," I tell him honestly, and he growls.

"Have you learned nothing?"

"I don't appreciate your tone," I say, and then I yelp as he turns me, glowering down into my face.

"I cannot leave my camp again. Already I will have to deal with the repercussions."

"So don't."

"If you go, karja, I will go too. It will be this way until I'm dead and buried."

I snarl at that, and he slides his hand in my hair, pulling my face close to his.

"You have been pulling away from me since we found your friend. Tell me why."

"Look, Rakiz, we're both tired—"

"Stop. What has happened?"

"I can't talk about it yet. Can you just hold me? Please?"

His brow lowers, and he pulls me even closer. I *hate* that even now, all I want to do is nuzzle into him and hear him tell me that everything will be all right.

He leans down, and I press my lips to his before moving them to his cheek, his jaw, his neck. He leans his head down and bites lightly on the most sensitive part of my neck, right beneath my ear, dragging a moan from my throat.

Rakiz slides his hands under my butt and gets to his feet, gracefully managing to not slip in the bath even as my nails dig into his shoulders in alarm.

He laughs as I curse at him, and then he lets me slowly slide down his body before he grabs a fur, pressing it against every inch of me. His hands are gentle and tender, and I let out a shaky breath as he leans forward, catching a drop of water sliding down my breast with his mouth.

When we're both dry, he takes my hand and looks into my eyes for a long moment. Then he smiles. The same kind of smile he gave me when we were out in the wild, far from camp.

He leads me to his bed, and I crawl onto the furs, laughing at his choked growl as he enjoys the view. I'm not at all surprised when he follows me down, sliding one hand around my waist as he nips at the top of my ear.

His body covers me from head to toe, and I sigh in pleasure as he pushes my hair over my shoulder and kisses his way along my neck and down my back.

I can feel him hard and ready against my ass, and I push back teasingly, grinning at his rough growl.

When I turn my head, his eyes are so dark they appear almost black in the low light.

"Hurry up," I say, and then he's thrusting inside me. I cry out, pushing back to meet him, and he slides in even further until he's nestled deep, right where I need him.

He buries his hand in my hair and turns my head, taking my mouth in a rough kiss. And then he's moving in a fluid rhythm, each thrust making my hands grab at the fur beneath me.

He slips one hand down low to where we're joined, caressing my clit in time with his strokes.

Just like that, I'm gasping, writhing in pleasure as my whole body shudders. I feel him tense behind me as a hoarse groan leaves his throat, and then we both fall boneless onto the furs.

Rakiz

Nevada sighs, moving closer to me, and I stroke her hair. In sleep, she knows that she belongs to me. Awake? That is a different story.

Never did I imagine that an alien female would one day be my mate. But from the moment I met this small human, it was like my life suddenly had color again. She may have made me want to pull out my hair, but she also made me laugh more than anyone I've ever met. And she made me want her until I thought I would die wanting her.

I thought she felt the same. But I have felt her slowly pulling away. Her body responds to mine, but her mind is elsewhere, and her nonanswers make me want to roar with frustration.

Nevada shifts and blinks her eyes open, staring up at me. For a moment, her lips curl into a smile, and then it's as if she remembers something, and that hint of a smile disappears.

"I need to get moving," she says, and I pull her closer.

"First, we need to talk."

"Rakiz—"

I won't risk her attempting to leave again. "By now you

know who I am, karja. Tell me, do you believe I can get your friends back to you?"

She's silent for a long moment. "I believe you can. I believe I can. But if we're not out there…"

"Think about Hewex and Tagiz. They fought long and hard with us. But any of my warriors would do the same. I need you to promise not to leave."

She's silent again, and I grit my teeth.

"I need to think about it," she says.

I resist the urge to growl. Once Nevada has given her word, she won't break it. I know this about her. So I will allow her time to think.

"I need to go check on Zoey," she says, and I allow her to roll away. She reaches for her pack, pulling out some clean pants, and I almost groan as she pulls them over her toned thighs and ass.

"I have a proposition for you," I say, the words spilling from my mouth before I can take them back.

"What kind of proposition?" Nevada places her hands on her hips, and I grin at the sight of my female warrior dressed only in leather, her breasts bare as she scowls at me.

I open my mouth, and she narrows her eyes at me.

"I don't have time for that proposition."

I grin, and her mouth twitches as she turns and reaches for a shirt.

"I want you to help secure the camp."

Nevada's hand freezes, and she tilts her head as she stares at me.

Yes, I know exactly how to entice you to stay with me, karja.

"What do you mean?"

I push back the furs and reach for my own pants. "As you pointed out, if it was easy for you to sneak out of this camp, it could be easy for others to sneak in. My tribe can benefit from your expertise."

She studies me. "Are you just doing this to keep me out of trouble?"

I raise my eyebrow, not missing the way her gaze scans my body before returning to my face. It takes every ounce of my willpower not to pull her to me for a morning tumble.

"Karja, I am under no illusions when it comes to your ability to find trouble wherever you go. I simply thought you may enjoy helping ensure that the members of this tribe are protected."

"What would that look like?" She rolls her eyes at my silence. "I mean, do I have your permission to make any necessary changes?"

"Anything that involves changing the duties of my warriors should be run past Terex first. But I trust you will fix the problems that allowed you to steal my mishua and sneak out of this camp."

Nevada's face falls at the reminder of my mishua, and I reach out, pulling her close.

"I have no doubt that you will have my warriors begging for mercy," I tease her, and she grins up at me.

"Okay, you asked for it," she says. "I don't want to hear any whining when I start pointing out the holes in your security."

She throws me one last smile as she finishes pulling on her shirt and then her boots before striding out the door.

Nevada

Ellie is sitting by Zoey's side when I enter the healer's kradi. She jumps to her feet and throws her arms around me.

"You did it," she whispers. "You brought her back."

I feel my mouth twist. "Ivy and Beth are still missing."

"From what Tagiz said, they both managed to escape. Moni said Zoey would've died if you hadn't brought her back here in time."

I pull away and study Zoey. "She looks a little better."

Ellie grins and points to a corner of the kradi, where one of the healers is hunched over a table.

I stare. "Is that mold?"

Ellie's grin widens. "That's an antibiotic."

Barbarian penicillin. Who would've thought?

I examine Zoey's pale face. "Has she woken up yet?"

"Moni gave her something to make her sleep. She said her body needed to rest." Ellie pushes a strand of hair behind one ear, and I narrow my eyes.

"What's that on your wrist?"

Ellie blushes. "We were going to wait until you guys were back, but...well—"

I know what they are. I asked around when we first got here, and I noticed that some of the men—and women— wear gleaming gold bands around their wrists.

"Mating bands."

Ellie chews on her lip. "Yeah. I'm sorry we didn't wait for you guys. We just wanted to have the ceremony as soon as possible, and we figured we'd celebrate when you got back."

We stare at each other for a moment, and then I finally snap my mouth closed.

"You're...staying?"

She nods firmly. "I'm pregnant, Nevada. And even if I

wasn't, I'm happy here. I didn't want to be stolen from my life, but honestly, even if I wasn't with Terex, I'd want to stay on Agron. I fit in here."

"Pregnant. Wow. Congratulations."

She gives me a look, and I grin.

"I mean it. It's just a shock. I take off for a couple of weeks, and when I come back, you're mated and pregnant."

"I know. We would've waited, but we just didn't know how long you'd be, and with the baby—"

"You don't have to explain, Ellie. I'm happy for you guys. You're going to be an amazing mother."

"I'm still going to help you guys get back to Earth. You know that, right?"

"Of course."

"So," she says, a tiny smile playing around her lips, "what happened when Rakiz went after you?"

I grin. "He lost his shit. But honestly, he wanted to be out there just as much as I did. I feel sorry for him—he's a warrior who loves hunting and fighting, but he's stuck ruling this tribe. Did you know he's funny? He was a completely different person away from camp."

"You know, people were saying he'd changed before he left. They were saying he smiled more, and he was taking more of an interest in life. Because of you."

I scowl. "It would never work anyway. I'm leaving, and he's the tribe king."

I take a seat next to Zoey, and Ellie moves closer.

"What's that got to do with anything?"

"He'll need a queen one day."

Ellie eyes me. "Would you want to be queen?"

"No. But Rakiz never wanted to be king. You know the crazy thing? I'd do it. I'd stay on this planet and be his queen if it meant I could be with him. But his tribe would never accept me. Right before I left, I told one of his councilors to go fuck himself," I say, and Ellie snorts.

"To be fair, that guy had it coming."

I try out a smile, but it's shaky. "I met his ex, Ellie. She's beautiful and sad, and she lives all alone in the armpit of this world because she couldn't stand the thought of watching him take a queen that would be worthy of ruling beside him." I scoff. "And I get it. There's no way I'd hang around for that either."

"Have you talked to him about this?"

I sigh. "I can't. What am I going to say? 'Oh, I know you already hate being king, and you're only doing it 'cause you're the best person for the job, but I'm going to cut this relationship off at the knees, since I can't be your queen. Even though I don't even want to be fucking queen, I just want you. All to myself. Forever.' Sounds great, doesn't it?"

She smiles. "Well, the last part sounds good. You may need to work on the first part."

"It's going to end eventually. Maybe it's better to just end it now before either of us get hurt any more."

Ellie raises her eyebrows at me silently, and I sigh again, feeling the sudden need to hit something.

"I'm going to go see if Asroz is around for training. Oh, I forgot to tell you. I'm the new head of security." I grin, and Ellie raises her eyebrow. "If the people around here don't like me now," I say, "they're really gonna hate me in a few days."

CHAPTER FIFTEEN

N*evada*

"So once the sentry sees someone coming, they need to ride back to the camp and scream at people until they prepare the defenses?"

Terex nods. "Yes."

He's a man of few words, but I see a gleam of humor in his eyes at my question.

"That's why the sentries can't be too far from camp?"

"In times of war, we have even more sentries. The ones posted furthest away will ride until they find a sentry posted closer to camp, and then he will ride, and so on."

Like a barbarian relay.

The problem? Once someone has spotted trouble on the horizon, that trouble is almost on top of them. And unless their enemies are total morons, they'll take out the sentry and prevent him from getting closer to camp.

I puzzle over it for a few hours, and then I talk to the

sentries. Some of them are still pissy that I managed to get past them, and others don't believe that a female should have anything to do with camp security.

When the third sentry sneers at me, I lose my patience.

I head straight to Terex, who tilts his head when I tell him what I want to do.

The meeting takes place in the meadow behind camp. There's no other place large enough for me to address so many warriors. I've got all the guards here, most of the sentries, and anyone else who's responsible for keeping the camp secure in any capacity.

I glance toward the back of the crowd and glower at the dark eyes laughing back at me. This would be easier without Rakiz watching.

He gives me a thumbs-up.

Smartass.

I turn away to hide my laugh, and then I climb up onto a table. The crowd goes quiet—most likely because they're shocked and curious.

"Okay," I say. "I'm not going to waste your time telling you why I'm qualified to talk to you about security. You know nothing about my planet or what I did on it, and you don't care. I get it. It's fine."

A few chuckles. I take a deep breath and go on.

"But here's what I know. Not long ago, I snuck out of here with food, weapons, and clothes. I made it into your weapons kradi, and I stole the king's mishua. I know," I say as mutters sound, "dick move. But there's a reason I'm telling you this. Every single person in this camp knew I was not to be trusted. You knew that on the king's orders, I wasn't to leave the camp at all. And yet I got out. Honestly, it was child's play. I'm not from this planet, and I know nothing about how life works here, and I had a plan within a few days."

Complete silence. I have their attention now.

"I don't say this to shame anyone. All I want to do is show you what I learned during this time and how the people in this camp can be safer. Because if I can sneak out...who could sneak in?"

A warrior named Jaris snorts and stares me down. He's never liked me, and I'm not at all surprised that he's the one to speak up.

"Why would we trust you? It's because of you that our king left."

I meet Rakiz's gaze, and his eyes aren't laughing anymore as his gaze lingers on Jaris's back.

"Is that who you think your king is? A man so easily swayed by my charms"—I gesture at my baggy shirt and dirty pants—"that he's unable to think for himself?"

The crowd goes silent, and Jaris finally shakes his head even as he glowers at me. To imply that his king is weak would be seen as a challenge, and Jaris isn't stupid enough to go up against Rakiz.

I glance up at the emerald sky. *Help me out here, Jack. What should I do?*

I can almost hear him, standing beside me, that cocky grin on his face.

They want to act like assholes? Make them look like assholes.

I smile, letting my gaze sweep the crowd. "You know what? I can't help you if you don't want help. But I'm going to prove to you that this camp isn't as secure as you think it is. In five days, we'll meet back here, and you can look me in the eyes and tell me that everything is fine."

Then I jump off my table and stride through the crowd.

Terex catches up to me. "You wanted them to challenge you."

"Oh yeah. Show, don't tell. Now they get to be beaten by a girl. And they asked for it."

He laughs. "I look forward to seeing what you come up with."

I stride straight to Rakiz's hut and wait for him.

He finds me sitting outside the door. "Scared of Arana?"

"She's still pissed at me for leaving."

He laughs, and I get to my feet, telling him what I want. I have people to help me with most of this stuff, but this is going to be my masterpiece.

He narrows his eyes at me. "I hope you're sure about this."

I shrug. "I have some experience with stubborn men. I can tell them all the problems I've seen, and they'll simply shrug their shoulders and ignore me because I'm a woman and I'm an outsider. But if I make them *see* those problems, they can't ignore me. Plus, this is way more satisfying, and in this place, I have to take my wins where I find them."

Rakiz laughs again. "You know, Terex or I could *make* them listen."

I shake my head. "What fun would that be?"

He reaches out and pulls me close, and every part of me wants to follow him into his hut and shut out the world. He brushes my mouth with his, and my eyes sting at his gentle touch.

"You stayed away last night," he murmurs.

I attempt a smile. "I slept in the healer's kradi with Zoey."

"Will you stay with me tonight?"

God, I want to. I want to so bad. "I don't think it's a good idea."

He pulls away, expression dark. "Why?"

"Rakiz..."

He frowns at me, and I sigh.

"Things are different now."

"They're not different at all. I'm your male, and you're my female. At least I thought you were."

"I am. I was." I blow out another breath, frustration making my hands shake. "Jesus, Rakiz, you're not an idiot. Whatever we're doing...it can't continue here at camp. You're the fucking tribe king, for God's sake."

"Finally, you tell me the problem. You think I didn't notice how you changed after we left Inexa's?"

I throw up my hands and step away. "She could be me, Rakiz!"

He growls and opens his door before pulling me into the hut. Arana is nowhere to be seen, and he scowls at me.

"Inexa could never be you."

"Why? Because she'd slept with a few of your friends and I haven't?"

He frowns. "What?"

"She knew she'd never be acceptable as your queen."

This time it's Rakiz who throws up his hands with a roar. "I was never even thinking about taking a queen!"

I nod. "I know. And you're not thinking now, but one day you will. One day you'll need to settle down and pick a woman for life. You'll need..." My throat closes, and I take a deep breath, fighting for control as Inexa's words come back to me. Again. "You'll need a queen that is well-mannered, popular among the tribe, and ready to bear you heirs. She will sit by your side and smile at your people and be your perfect match in every way."

If I wasn't breaking my own heart, the expression on

Rakiz's face would be comical. His mouth hangs open for a moment before he snaps it closed with a snarl.

"This is what you think? That I will take a well-mannered female? Karja, after being with you, I can think of nothing worse."

I'm so close to tears that I can't stand it, and I need to get out of here before I fall apart. "Everyone I've ever loved has either left me or died, Rakiz. I can't take any more."

He opens his mouth, and I hold up my hand, backing away a step. "You'll do your duty. As you have your whole life. And I get it. These people rely on you. You're a man of honor. So...we need to just be friends."

Friends.

The word is like ash on my tongue, and for the first time since shortly after I arrived here, Rakiz's eyes turn cold. When he looks at me, it's always with fury, lust, impatience, or humor but never this blank stare as if we're strangers. I choke back a sob as I bolt for the door.

He doesn't try to stop me from leaving.

***

Rakiz

My hellion has turned my camp upside down. Each day my warriors come to complain about her tricks and demonstrations, and each day I fight the urge to haul her back to my tashiv.

On the first day, two of our strongest, most reliable mishua went missing. They were later found inside Jaris's kradi. His roar of outrage could be heard throughout the camp.

On the second day, someone handed a sentry a piece of

fruit that had been laced with some kind of fast-acting sleep tonic. When he woke, he'd been stripped naked and tied to the camp entrance.

I struggled to contain my smile when I saw him glaring daggers at Nevada as she walked by, ignoring him.

On the third day, all of the training swords in the weapons kradi were replaced with white sticks from a clump of trees close to our camp.

By the fourth day, I assigned Nevada a guard. Hewex was to follow her throughout the camp, the grizzled warrior leveling his stare on anyone who thought to voice their annoyance about her actions.

My karja is right about one thing—this camp must be made as secure as possible.

Today is the fifth day, and I'm currently watching Nevada train with Asroz in the arena as they ignore the crowd that gathered to watch them fight.

Nevada has come a long way, and her skills with a sword have some of my warriors raising their eyebrows and nodding their heads in respect even as others turn and stalk away, disgusted at the sight of a female fighting.

Nevada couldn't care less.

If she truly wanted to be queen, she would talk about pleasant things with these people. She would wear a dress and smile at my warriors and hold her tongue.

I have seen that behavior before.

What Inexa obviously failed to mention to my karja is that it wasn't because of how she acted when we were first together that kept me away from camp for longer and longer periods.

It was when we had been tumbling for some time, and she slowly began to change from the funny, interesting female I had known into the female she thought that the tribe would want her to be.

She no longer told bawdy jokes or even spoke with the other warriors. She spent more and more time with the healers, speaking of female things—things she had never been interested in before.

Eventually, she was almost unrecognizable from the female I had known...and come close to mating.

She had changed for the tribe, but they saw her actions as manipulative and calculated.

Inexa leaving the tribe was one of my greatest failures. Not just because of the way she changed but because the loss of any female when there are so few is something to be mourned.

"I beg of you, Rakiz. Let me go and live my life. You owe me this."

I did owe her that. If I hadn't been tribe king, if my father hadn't been making it clear that I should be taking a mate, if I had paid more attention when her smiles became false and she began agreeing with everything I said...

I scowl.

"She's getting good."

I turn at the voice and nod as Terex stands next to me, his gaze on the training arena.

"The fight is in her blood."

"She no longer sleeps in your tashiv."

I turn my head, and Terex raises his eyebrows.

"People talk."

I feel my scowl deepen. "She doesn't want to be with me. She says I'll end up taking a queen, and she doesn't want to watch it happen."

"Sounds like Inexa."

"Inexa spoke to her. We were good before that. I'd never been happier."

"I'm surprised the hellion listened to anything someone else had to say."

"Everyone I've ever loved has either left me or died, Rakiz. I can't take any more."

"She has been wounded. Her life was one of incredible loss. She didn't come to me whole, and I accepted that."

Terex snorts. "After so many females desperate to be the tribe queen, who would have thought you'd fall in love with the one who wants nothing to do with the title?"

Love. "Is that what this is?"

Terex sends me a pitying look. "You know how the tribe gossips. You've gone from finally smiling and actually caring about more than just hunting the Voildi to a man with moods so dark even your councilors are afraid to approach you. Sounds like love to me."

I watch Nevada as Asroz lunges, and she darts out of reach. She jolts forward and smacks him on the ass with her training sword, and I chuckle as he throws her a black look.

"She's not doing well either," Terex tells me softly. "Ellie said she's staying with the other female—Vivian. Apparently she's no longer sleeping."

I rub my chest at the thought of my hellion crying out in her sleep. And then I straighten my shoulders as Nevada glances up at us, meeting my gaze for a moment before she looks away.

My female has never been easy, but she is worth the fight. She is worth everything.

Nevada

What do I do when my life is falling apart and I want nothing more than to get on my knees and beg the tribe king for a scrap of his attention?

Torture his entire tribe.

They're pissed. But things are about to get a whole lot worse.

I've had a lot of time on my hands. Sleepless nights when I cried into my pillow as soon as Vivian had fallen asleep.

Me. Nevada. Crying over a man. It would be funny if it wasn't so fucking embarrassing.

I thought that it would hurt less—that it'd be easier for both of us if we just called it quits now. I can focus on finding the other women so we can get back to Earth, and he can focus on ruling his tribe.

But I can't imagine anything hurting more than this.

I sigh and roll over in my furs. Vivian gave me a look when I moved in here and asked when her kradi became the "designated breakup tent," but her expression softened when she took a good look at my face. "You can have Alexis's bed. The pillow's probably still damp from when Ellie cried all over it."

Vivian's already up today. While I'm tempted to roll back over and cry myself back to sleep, I need to get up so I can put the final phase of Operation Undermine Camp Security into effect.

First, I check on Zoey. Her eyes blink open when I walk in, and a smile crosses her face.

I grin, relief hitting me like a punch in the gut. At least one thing is okay. Ellie looks up and matches my grin, gesturing to the plate of food Zoey's nibbling on.

"How are you feeling?" I ask.

"Like I survived pneumonia. With the alien version of antibiotics."

I laugh, and I'm so fucking relieved and exhausted and sad that I fall to my knees next to her bed, bury my face in her furs, and burst into tears.

"Oh my God," Ellie says, wrapping her arm around me. "Are you okay?"

I choke out a laugh. "Zoey's the one on her deathbed, and you're asking if I'm okay?"

"Well you're kind of having a breakdown," Zoey says, and I grin even as I wipe tears off my face.

"I'm sorry."

"Don't apologize. From what Ellie says, you've been holding everyone together. You're entitled to have a cry every now and again."

"I just had one last night. And the night before."

Ellie reaches out and strokes my hair back from my face, and the action is so maternal that another tear slips down my cheek.

"Well," she says. "Maybe you're long overdue."

"I lost him," I murmur. "I let him go, and I lost him."

"Have you talked to him?"

I shake my head and finally sit up. Zoey's eyes are wet with sympathy, and we all turn as Moni enters the kradi.

She takes one look at me and tuts before handing me a plate of food. "Take it, child. Don't argue with an old woman."

I force a smile onto my face and take the plate. Moni looks at me for a long moment, and we're all silent.

Then she speaks. "If he could reply, he would tell you to take your happiness wherever you can fucking find it."

My mouth drops open, and Ellie shifts beside me.

"Who?" she asks. "Rakiz?"

Moni shakes her head with a smile and walks back out.

I'm still staring at where she was standing when Ellie pushes my plate closer to me.

"The Braxians don't curse like us. They use Brax words."

"Yeah," I say. "They do. Sorry, guys, I've got to go. I'll be back later."

I'm satisfied with the dirty looks thrown my way as I move within the camp. If people are annoyed, it means they're taking notice. Real change comes when people have no choice but to examine their weaknesses.

Still, they're going to be really annoyed by what I have planned next.

I glance at Terex, who nods at me from where he's standing near the mishua pen. Everything is ready to go. Excellent.

BOOM!

The explosion is small, but even I flinch as the kradi blows. Screams sound, and if I wasn't in the worst mood of my life, I'd probably feel bad.

Instead, I watch as everything I predicted happens as if according to a script. All the warriors who are in the training arena instantly run toward the explosion. At least two sentries leave their posts completely, desperate to see what's happened, and chaos reigns.

When I told Terex what I wanted to do, he immediately shook his head, but I saw the interest in his eyes when I explained why. The kids have all been safely hidden away, and both Terex and Rakiz ensured that no one would be anywhere near the kradi when it blew.

When we attacked the Voildi's lair, Tagiz used twelve pods to create his explosion. For this, I've used just one. I'm not aiming for destruction. Just the sound and sight of something burning even as Terex immediately puts out the small flames.

All eyes turn to me as I walk up, and most of them are enraged.

I've managed to antagonize an entire tribe of alien warriors. *Good work, Nevada.*

A strong arm wraps around me, grabbing my hand as I tense and reach for my sword. Rakiz's scent hits me, leather and warrior. He pulls me close, and I look up at his face, but his gaze is scanning all the warriors staring at me until, one by one, they glance away.

I frown at him. By now, he should know that I don't need to be rescued. But my heart still skips a beat as he strokes his finger lightly across my hand and then moves away. Even now, when he can't even bear to look at me, he still has my back.

I move away, eyes forward. The warriors know where to find me now.

It doesn't take long for them to find their way to the meadow. I stand on the same table, watching as they arrive. Rakiz appears, but no one approaches him, preferring to stare at me as if I'm a serial killer they've found hiding in their midst.

Ellie arrives, her hand in Terex's. She raises her other arm, giving me a thumbs-up, and I blow out a shaky breath as I avoid Rakiz's gaze. Was it really just five days ago that we ended?

I glance at a robed figure on the outskirts of the crowd, and then I get straight to business.

"Over the past five days, I've tested the security of this camp. While you'd be forgiven for assuming otherwise, it brings me no pleasure to expose some of the complacency

I've found in that security." I smile slightly. "Okay, it brings me a little pleasure."

A few laughs sound, and I take a deep breath.

"While I'm not from this tribe, or even from this planet, I know a few things. I know that three years ago, the Evix tribe was wiped out when they were infiltrated by their enemies. I know a pack of Voildi who are big-picture thinkers and managed to collaborate long enough to kidnap my friends, hide them, and find buyers. And I know that sometimes life sucks. Sometimes you think you're safe only to lose the ones you love."

My voice cracks, and I brush away a tear before it can fall.

"That happened to me. And I don't want it to happen to any of you. That's why I'm doing this. Not because I want you to look like idiots, although that was a fun bonus. But because this tribe can do better."

I gesture to the cloaked figure, and he steps forward. Gasps sound, and swords are drawn as the warrior throws off his hood and grins at me.

Apparently Dexar was amused by our request. Amused enough that when we managed to get word to him through one of his hunting parties, he decided to let us borrow one of his warriors for this little display.

The guy doesn't seem at all afraid, even surrounded by a tribe of growling warriors. Balls of steel.

"That explosion could have happened simultaneously around our camp. All it would take is for those pods to be snuck in with the food. When the kradi flew into the air, almost every single one of you ran toward it. I know you were likely making sure there were no women or children hurt. But this distraction allowed an enemy warrior to sneak in. Your sentries were away from their posts, making it easy for a tribe to take us unaware. Imagine what one enemy could do while hidden within this camp. And imagine if he brought friends. Imagine if that distraction was a way to keep you busy while the enemy rode on your camp."

The warriors are listening intently now, and I feel my shoulders relax slightly.

"Will you allow me to offer you a few suggestions? Suggestions that will help to keep every man, woman, and child safe in this camp and future camps?"

Asroz drops to one knee, bowing his head in a show of support. Hewex and Tagiz immediately follow, and at least ten other warriors do the same. One or two spin and stalk away, while the rest keep their arms folded but nod at me.

I'll take it.

CHAPTER SIXTEEN

N*evada*

I KEEP MYSELF BUSY. MOST DAYS, I TEACH SMALL GROUPS OF warriors how to track without their noses. I make them stuff scented material in their nostrils, and then they compete to find each other through the forest nearby.

The search for Ivy and Beth continues, and Terex gives me updates whenever he has new information.

From what I can understand, all the Braxian tribes must have originally been related in some way. Some of them have alliances, others have trade deals, and some at least have a kind of truce—like the one between Rakiz and Dexar. Then there are those that will kill each other on sight.

A human woman with flame-colored hair was apparently seen running into the territory of a Braxian tribe that doesn't have any truce or alliance with Rakiz's tribe.

Rakiz has sent some of his warriors to the area to see if they can spot any sign of Ivy.

Beth is still nowhere to be seen.

And Charlie? All we know is what the blue man told us, and Rakiz has also sent warriors to attempt to trace the dragon's footsteps.

Of course, I'm getting all of this information second-hand, since I'm too much of a coward to talk to Rakiz, no matter what I said about "friendship".

I push the thought of the tribe king out of my head and focus on Geris—one of the sentries. He's raising his eyebrow at me, and I nod.

"Do it."

We're probably about a thousand feet from camp. Asroz came with me, and he's watching with interest from his mishua.

Geris picks up the long rope, which has been made from some kind of flax-like plant. It's incredibly strong and attached to a bell located by the next closest sentry on this side. When his bell rings, he'll pull his own rope, which will ring the next bell, and so on.

We wait, breathlessly, and just a few seconds later...

Ring, ring, ring.

We all grin as the huge bell located in the training arena sounds, alerting the entire camp.

We've placed these ropes surrounding the camp in all directions. The goal is to extend them out even further so the moment a potential invader gets within a mile of the camp, our sentries will alert the warriors to be ready.

"This is very well done," Asroz says quietly.

I smile up at him, but we're both aware that Rakiz should be here for this. I'm not sure where he is, but I haven't seen him in days.

I feel like a hypocrite. Each night it takes every ounce of my willpower to not leave my kradi and make my way to his tashiv, where I'll fall on my knees and beg him to take me back.

The only thing stopping me? The thought of what would happen next.

I can't believe I was dumb enough to fall in love with the tribe king. My stomach clenches as I stare into the distance. Because that's what this must be. *Breakup* is too mild of a word for what this is. This is a shock wave through everything I ever thought I knew and all my plans for the future.

It's a good thing Rakiz is nowhere to be seen. Because if he was close by...

I'd make a fool of myself begging for him to take me back.

"Here." Asroz offers me his hand. "Let's go."

It feels weird to ride on a mishua in front of a man that's not Rakiz. We're quiet as we slowly head back to camp, and I feel the sudden urge to take the mishua and run.

"Are you okay?"

I blink. Asroz and I don't talk about anything "girlie" like *feelings*. I think the only way he can train me is to imagine that I'm actually a male.

"Not really," I admit. "But I will be. One day."

Hopefully.

One of the sentries scans us when we arrive.

"The king has called a breen," he says, and Asroz tenses behind me.

"What's a breen?"

"A meeting of the whole tribe," Asroz says. "Only sentries and the very sick are permitted to not attend."

Butterflies instantly become a swarm in my stomach. Surely no one would notice if I wasn't there, right?

"Don't even think about it."

I sigh. Asroz is one hell of a hard-ass sometimes.

We leave the mishua in the pen, and her eyes turn heavy-lidded as Asroz gives her a stroke. Then I follow Asroz to the meadow—the only place large enough for a meeting of this size.

Even then, it's a stretch.

There are thousands of people in this tribe. Granted, many warriors are currently away on various orders, but it's still a tight squeeze. I find Ellie close to the front, and I elbow my way through the crowd until I can whisper in her ear.

"Any idea what this is about?"

Ellie shakes her head. "Apparently it's very rare to call a breen. It's not something that's usually done without a lot of advance notice."

People are murmuring in low voices, but those murmurs begin to die down. I turn to see the crowd parting for Rakiz, who meets my gaze for a split second before he stands on a raised dais that wasn't here earlier.

Rakiz's councilors follow in his wake. They're older men who no longer fight as warriors, and they're the bane of his existence. Every single one of them looks like they've been sucking on a lemon, and more than one sends me a furious glance.

"What the hell?" I murmur, and I feel Ellie shrug beside me.

Rakiz stares over the crowd. His eyes are shadowed, and my heart aches. All I want is for us to hide away somewhere remote and shut out the world.

"Thank you for joining me here today. I'll keep this short. This is something that I have wanted for a long time, but I wasn't brave enough to do it."

Whispers sound, people voicing their shock at his admission.

"I will be stepping down as king. I know this is unexpected, but I will make this transition as easy as possible."

What. The. Fuck.

Before I know it, I'm shoving my way forward, ignoring the filthy looks aimed my way as gasps sound across the crowd.

"What are you doing?" I demand, and the old woman next to me holds her hand to her chest, blood draining from her face as if she might actually faint.

"You won't be with me as king. So now I'm just a male."

I grind my teeth. "You didn't want to talk to me about this?"

Rakiz sighs. "I'm not used to compromising. I'm not someone who shares. I'll do my best to include you in my decisions, but sometimes those decisions will be mine to make."

I examine him. He's actually fucking serious about this. He's giving up everything.

"And just what does this decision look like?"

The crowd is deathly quiet, and Rakiz reaches down, pulling me up onto the dais with him.

"We will have to leave. I can't stay here—it would be an insult to the next king. But we will have our own life, our own adventures. I will make you happy, Nevada."

I blink back tears. "Why would you do this?"

"If you stay with me, you'll be giving up your home for me. I want you to be my mate. To be the mother of my children."

The tribe is currently going nuts. Warriors are roaring in outrage, women are crying, and Rakiz only has eyes for me.

"I'm not taking you away from your tribe. They need you."

"Not as much as I need you."

For the first time, Rakiz is putting his needs before the tribe. And it's killing him. I can see it in the hard lines of his face, in the way he keeps his eyes on me, ignoring the outcry from his tribe.

I did this.

"You're not doing it."

"Karja, I already have."

"No." I turn to the crowd. "Your king is staying here."

"Nevada—"

"But he's mine," I continue. "Forever. I'm not giving him back. And if anyone has a problem with that, you can suck it. He's given his whole life to this tribe, and for once he's going to have what he wants. For some crazy reason, what he wants is me. So until he changes his mind, I'll be hanging around."

Relief shows on the faces staring up at us. I've drawn my line in the sand, and they're so desperate to keep Rakiz that they'll even take me with him.

I turn and eye him. "You're a master manipulator," I mutter, and his eyes light with humor. "Would you really have left?"

Rakiz pulls me close, his gaze intent. "Karja, I've already packed my bags. I'd leave in a heartbeat. But something told me I wouldn't have to."

I shake my head even as I laugh. I should be more annoyed at being played like a violin, but I'm just so fucking relieved to have him back that I don't even care if he just managed to manipulate me along with thousands of other people.

Somehow he snuck under all my defenses. I'm leaving my life on Earth behind, and yet I no longer feel like I'm giving up anything. Instead, I feel like I'm gaining everything.

"I love you. Even though you're an arrogant ass."

"I love you too. Even though you're a stubborn hellion."

I grin up at him. He's possessive, paranoid, and controlling, and he's not happy unless he gets things his way. I'm demanding, pissy, and headstrong, and I'm not happy unless I get things *my* way.

But somehow we work.

Rakiz leans down and takes my mouth. Then he drops to his knees and reaches into his pocket, pulling out two gold bands.

I swallow around the lump in my throat as he looks up at me solemnly and hands them to me.

"I thought I was supposed to make these bands."

He smiles. "I'm not taking any chances." He holds out his arms, and his face is solemn as I tie one around each wrist, my hands shaking.

Then I squeak as he picks me up and jumps off the dais before striding through the crowd and back toward his tashiv.

The camp is silent and empty—everyone still back at the meadow, likely discussing what's just happened. I'm still in shock as I stare up at my warrior, and only the warm feel of his skin under my hand as I stroke his cheek convinces me that I'm not dreaming.

He glances down at me, and then he curses as I lean up and press kisses along his jaw, causing him to stumble.

I laugh, giddy with happiness as he slides me a look and one side of his mouth curls up.

Moments later, he opens the door to the tashiv and stalks in, kicking it closed and then heading straight to his furs. He puts me down, and I blink up at him for a moment, my eyes adjusting to the dim light as my throat goes dry under the heated focus of his gaze.

It feels like my skin is too tight for my body as he slowly leans down, his eyes on mine.

"Kiss me," I murmur, and he gives me a slow smile. Then I'm gasping as his quick fingers undo my shirt and pull it over my head. He picks me up again and lays me on the furs, and then he stares down at me for a long moment, his gaze scanning my body.

I shiver at the promise in his eyes, and then he leans down again. Just when I think he's finally going to kiss me, he pulls off my pants, leaving me naked and waiting for him.

"Planning to come closer?" I ask. He continues to look at me with his dark eyes, and I blink back tears as our eyes meet again.

His gaze is full of...love. If I hadn't believed his words in the meadow, the way he looks at me now—as if he can't quite believe I'm here—would convince me of his truthfulness. Somehow the perfect man for me turned out to be an alien warrior tribe king. Who would've thought?

"I'm getting bored waiting for you," I tease, and he raises an eyebrow as he finally pulls off his boots. I run my hands up to my breasts, palming them as his gaze turns burning hot.

"Keep going," he orders, and I send him a grin but nod at his shirt.

"Take it off."

He rips off his shirt, and I roll my nipples, gasping as they ache for his touch. He pauses, standing before me, his huge muscled chest a temptation I can't ignore.

"Come closer," I say, and he raises one eyebrow, gesturing for me to keep going.

I grin at him but slide one hand down between my legs.

Rakiz growls, and within moments he has shucked off

his pants, and he kneels in front of me, pushing my hand to the side and replacing it with his mouth.

"God, you're good at that."

My head falls back as he licks my pussy—one long sweep of his tongue that makes me shudder. His tongue moves up to circle my clit, and I glance down, almost coming at the sight of his dark head between my pale thighs.

He pauses, ignoring my protest, and looks up, meeting my gaze with a wicked grin. And then he moves up and flips me onto my stomach before guiding me up to my knees. He pushes my thighs further apart, and then his mouth is on me again, teasing and stroking as I bury my hands in the soft fur.

"Rakiz..."

He pushes one finger into me, and I clench around it, gasping as he teases my clit while caressing my G-spot.

"You tease," I groan as he dances over my pussy, his huge hands on my thighs holding me open for him as I writhe, attempting to move closer.

"It's been many nights since I've had my hellion in my bed," he murmurs before his mouth returns to where I need him the most.

"So what?" I gasp. "This is punishment?"

"This is me enjoying my karja."

There isn't much I can say to that, but I moan as he lavishes attention on my clit, finally adding another finger inside me and thrusting as he uses the very edge of his teeth.

I see stars.

My orgasm blinds me, my entire body shuddering as Rakiz holds tight, drawing my orgasm out, on and on until I slump on my stomach, completely wrecked.

I crack open one eye as Rakiz rolls me onto my back again, his expression tight and his cheekbones flushed with arousal.

Lust flutters in my belly again as I take in his well-muscled chest, golden skin, and heavy, thick cock. I meet his dark gaze, and then he's positioning himself at my entrance, taking me with a hard thrust into my swollen pussy, immediately priming me for another orgasm.

His rhythm is demanding, but it's the heat in his eyes, the love written all over his face that tips me over. I shatter into a million pieces, and then I'm rebuilt in his arms, completely possessed by my alien warrior. He groans as he reaches his own pleasure, and I smile as my eyes slide closed.

N*evada*

"Come on, baby, is that all you've got?" I tease.

Rakiz sends me a filthy grin, and then I'm darting back as his training sword slashes toward me. He refused to use the blunt metal training swords with me, insisting instead that we use the wooden swords that the kids train with.

Still, I wouldn't be surprised if he could take someone's head off with his sheer strength and skill, even with a wooden sword.

Sigh.

He leans forward, and the move is almost lazy as his sword suddenly appears at my throat.

"Point."

Damn it.

I scowl, and his grin widens. For someone who wasn't too pleased with my pants and sword, he sure seems to be enjoying them both now.

Rakiz's dark gaze scans my body, and I raise an eyebrow. Then we're moving again, and I grimace as he slides under my guard *again*, his sword poking me in the ribs.

"Point."

I whirl away, checking the sidelines. For once no one is around. We snuck out before dawn to have this time to ourselves. Ruling a tribe never stops, but we've vowed to make time for each other no matter what.

With a quick flick of my wrist, I undo the strings holding my shirt together as I turn. I don't think this is what Asroz had in mind when he taught me to fight dirty, but sometimes it pays to think outside the box.

I roll my shoulders and suppress a grin as I feel the strings loosen. Then I thrust, ready for Rakiz to casually sweep my sword aside. I sidestep, and a breeze hits my chest.

Excellent.

We circle, and then Rakiz attacks in a whirl that I barely dodge. The worst part? He's going easy on me. I grind my teeth at the thought, but my next shrug opens my shirt enough that Rakiz's gaze immediately drops to my chest.

"What?" I ask, adding a frown for good measure.

I hold my sword higher, and feel my nipples harden at both the cool air and the heat in Rakiz's eyes.

He glances around, checking we're alone.

"You play to win, karja."

I sniff. "I don't know what you're talking about."

Rakiz jolts forward, and this time, the sweep of his sword is meant to disarm me. He must think I was born yesterday. I duck beneath his arm, and my left breast pops out of my shirt.

Oops.

"Nevada," Rakiz roars, and I grin at him as I slide my sword underneath his armpit.

"Point."

I dart away, and Rakiz scowls, but amusement is clear in his eyes. He lunges forward, and in the blink of an eye, I'm trapped beneath him on the hard ground, his body surrounding me.

"You little cheat," he says, and his gaze drops to my lips as I smirk.

He leans down, and my heart beats faster. No one can make me feel like this but Rakiz. With him, life is an adventure.

"Nevada Lake! Just what do you think you're doing?"

Rakiz growls against my lips, and we both turn our heads as Ellie stalks toward us, hands on her hips.

"Uh-oh," I murmur. "Caught."

"Today's the day of your mating ceremony, and do I find you in the bath where you should be? No, I find you wrestling with your giant warrior in the mud."

I laugh and wiggle away from my giant warrior, who looks displeased. Ellie gives him a stern look.

"You'll be getting ready in our kradi with Terex. The tashiv is for Nevada."

Rakiz raises his eyebrows but shrugs.

"Thanks for the save," I mutter at him, and he sends me a wicked grin.

He jumps to his feet and leans forward, tying my shirt back up. "See you later...baby."

God, this man makes me hot.

I follow Ellie through the camp and back to our tashiv. Arana has forgiven me for leaving, although she made me work for it. There were no honey cakes for me until I swore to her I wouldn't suddenly take off again.

I'm going to be the tribe queen. So I'll use that power to find Charlie, Beth, and Ivy. According to Terex, Dexar is sticking to our agreement. He's got his warriors combing the region for the missing women, and the two tribes are sharing information.

I still don't trust him, and I wouldn't be surprised if he found one of the women and attempted to hide them in his tribe. But I have no doubt that Alexis would get a message back to us.

So far she's only sent one message saying she's safe and well and asking about our "status." I promised her we'd rescue her when we found the other women, and I keep my promises.

"There you are," Arana says as we walk in. "I have a bath ready for you. And here's your dress."

I raise my eyebrows, and Vivian snorts from where she's planted herself near the food.

"Since when does Nevada wear dresses?"

Ellie grins at me. "Since she wants to knock Rakiz's socks off. Come on, Nevada, it'll be such a good surprise! You know he won't be expecting it."

I examine the dress. If it was pink or purple, I'd immediately say no. But it's a deep blue, cut to show an underlayer the color of moonstones. It doesn't look flouncy or ridiculous, and it's missing some of the layers that make the dresses around here such a chore to wear.

It looks...regal. Without being stuffy.

"Who made this?"

"Terex's mom. She's a genius. Do you like it?"

"Surprisingly, yes. Okay, let's knock his socks off."

"Yay! Okay, get in the bath."

I obey, stripping off my muddy clothes and sliding into the warm water. I dunk my head, and then Arana steps in.

"Let me help."

I nod, and she cleans my hair before running a cool

liquid through it. Whatever she uses is magic, and it makes my thick, constantly tangled hair shiny and manageable.

Once I'm out of the bath, Vivian uses her own brand of magic to fuss with my face. While there are no real cosmetics here, the women get creative. Vivian uses a kohl-like substance to darken my eyes and the juice from a dark-red berry to stain my lips. Arana brushes out my hair and braids it while it's still damp so it will be curly for the ceremony.

Finally, what feels like hours later, I'm ready to step into my dress.

Ellie smiles at me, still slightly green. A servant brought in some cooked meat, and Ellie sprinted for the door to empty her stomach outside. I told her to lie down, but she wouldn't hear of it. Rakiz's mother comes to mind.

"You know you need to stay close to the healers, right? No taking off to do anything once you're showing."

"I know. I heard what happened to Rakiz's mom too, Nevada. I'll be careful, I promise. Now let's focus on you." Ellie picks up the dress, and I drop the fur I've had wrapped around me and step into it.

"I wish Zoey could've come."

"Same," I sigh. "But I'm just glad she's slowly getting better."

Tagiz has refused to leave her side and basically lives in the healer's tent now. Zoey is making noises about having a kradi of her own, but I'm pretty sure it'll be a few more weeks before that happens.

Ellie pulls up the dress and tightens the strings at the back. Arana steps forward and loosens my braid until my hair falls around my shoulders. Then she reaches for a gold circlet and places it on my head.

"Wow," Vivian says. "You look..."

"Like a queen," Ellie smiles. "Are you ready?"

"I'm nervous. Would you believe that?" I say.

"A few nerves are a good thing. Just tell me this: Is this what you want?"

I blow out a shaky breath, most of the nerves leaving me in a rush. "God, yes."

"Then let's do this."

We all file out of the tashiv, and my head is whirling as I walk through the camp. It's almost impossible to believe that I chose to leave everything I love about Earth behind and rule over a bunch of barbarian alien warriors. But these people have become my family. Somehow the worst experience of my life brought me to the man that makes my life complete.

Within moments we're in the meadow. Conversations stop, but I only have eyes for Rakiz, who turns his head, meeting my gaze.

His mouth drops open.

Socks. Off.

I grin at him, and he grins back, striding toward me.

"Karja. You look...there are no words."

Okay, the dress was worth it. Rakiz still looks slightly stunned, his gaze traveling up and down my body before pausing on the circlet.

"Later, when I claim your body, you will wear only that."

I blush, and Rakiz laughs, taking my hand and leading me to the front of the crowd. Usually people would arrive slowly, but it seems as if most of the tribe are already here, ready to see their king mated.

The ceremony is a blur. But I'll remember the look of promise on Rakiz's face until the day I die.

We move toward the fire, and Rakiz lets my hand go, taking his place. Terex steps forward, and I shake my head.

"It's okay," I say. "I've got this."

I gather the dress in one hand, and confused murmurs sound as I back away from the fire. Murmurs turn to gasps and shrieks as I sprint toward it, feet pounding as I launch high, flying over the fire before landing in Rakiz's arms.

Stunned silence.

I throw my head back and laugh, and Rakiz growls, taking my mouth even as his chest shakes with laughter. We pull apart as the crowd claps and cheers, and then Rakiz places me back on my feet, still holding me close.

Then he takes the golden bands from Terex's hand.

"Karja," he says, his voice hoarse. "I have made these bands to represent our bond. Strong, true, and never to be broken. Will you accept them?"

"I will."

Tears slide down my face as Rakiz ties the bands around my wrists, and then he's claiming my mouth in a preview of what will happen later. I feel my cheeks heat, and he lets out a low laugh as he pulls away.

We turn to the tribe, which bursts into applause. The cheers are deafening. Not because of the tribe's bonus ruler, I'm sure, but if I'm going to be queen of this tribe, I'll be the best queen I can be.

With my king by my side.

THE END

I hope you enjoyed Claimed by the Alien Warrior! Reviews help other readers find this series on Amazon, so if you have a few moments, I'd love if you could share your thoughts :)

Want to be the first to know about freebies, new releases

and audio? Head to hopehartauthor.com to sign up for my newsletter or follow me on Facebook.

Next up is Zarix and Beth's story in Saved by the Alien Warrior. Beth's about to prove that ballerina's are some of the toughest people around, all while coaxing smiles from a very grumpy warrior...

Happy reading!

Hope x